## From Megan Maitland's Diary

*Dear Diary,*

*I ran into Katie Topper in the nursery today. She looked a little tired, but thank goodness she's back from Houston. Ford Carrington simply hasn't been himself since she left. Of course, nothing has been sane around here since little Cody turned up on our doorstep! But I suppose gossip and scandal bring out the worst in people. Just look at all the women crawling out of the woodwork trying to claim that darling child. And now this Janelle person appears out of the blue, saying she's the mother, causing a scene!*

*It's all simply too much. I need time to think, time to decide what to do next. If what Janelle says is true... well, I just don't know. Could I <u>really</u> be that sweet baby's grandmother?*

Dear Reader,

There's never a dull moment at Maitland Maternity! This unique and now world-renowned clinic was founded twenty-five years ago by Megan Maitland, widow of William Maitland, of the prominent Austin, Texas, Maitlands. Megan is also matriarch of an impressive family of seven children, many of whom are active participants in the everyday miracles that bring children into the world.

When our series began, the family was stunned by the unexpected arrival of an unidentified baby at the clinic—unidentified, except for the claim that the child is a Maitland. Who are the parents of this child? Is the claim legitimate? Will the media's tenacious grip on this news damage the clinic's reputation? Suddenly rumors and counterclaims abound. Women claiming to be the child's mother are materializing out of the woodwork! How will Megan get at the truth? And how will the media circus affect the lives and loves of the Maitland children—Abby, the head of gynecology, Ellie, the hospital administrator, her twin sister, Beth, who runs the day-care center, Mitchell, the fertility specialist, R.J., the vice president of operations, even Anna, who has nothing to do with the clinic, and Jake, the black sheep of the family?

Please join us each month over the next year as the mystery of the Maitland baby unravels, bit by enticing bit, and book by captivating book!

Marsha Zinberg,
Senior Editor and Editorial Coordinator, Special Projects

# JULE McBRIDE

## Prescription: Baby

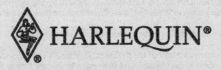

HARLEQUIN®

TORONTO • NEW YORK • LONDON
AMSTERDAM • PARIS • SYDNEY • HAMBURG
STOCKHOLM • ATHENS • TOKYO • MILAN • MADRID
PRAGUE • WARSAW • BUDAPEST • AUCKLAND

HARLEQUIN BOOKS
225 Duncan Mill Road, Don Mills,
Ontario, Canada M3B 3K9

ISBN 0-373-65066-3

PRESCRIPTION: BABY

Copyright © 2000 by Harlequin Books S.A.

Jule McBride is acknowledged as the author of this work.

Visit us at www.eHarlequin.com

**Printed in U.S.A.**

Jule McBride received the *Romantic Times* Reviewer's Choice Award for Best First Series Romance in 1993. Since then she has penned thirty more heartwarming love stories that have met with strong reviews, been nominated for awards and made repeated appearances on romance bestseller lists. A three-time Reviewer's Choice nominee for Best American Romance, Jule has also been nominated for two Lifetime Achievement awards in the category of Love and Laughter.

# CHAPTER ONE

DOCTOR FORD Freeland Carrington.

Seeing him outside the operating room could turn her face as red as her hair and her knees to water. If he passed her in a hallway or politely held open a door, cold sweat would break out above her lips, and if he should ever kiss her—outside her wickedest dreams—pediatric nurse Katie Topper feared her iron-clad constitution would give way and she'd drop into a dead faint like the Texas Southern belles she loved to hate.

For two years, she'd wanted Ford Carrington. She damn well respected him, too, but now she'd stooped to lusting after him while he was performing surgery. This was even worse than letting her mind stray to him during the Sunday services she sometimes attended with her papa, where Reverend Kenneth would work himself into a full lather, preaching hellfire and brimstone.

Hellfire Katie knew about of course. Her papa lovingly joked that more than the usual quota coursed through her Irish blood. It was probably why she couldn't keep her mind off Ford. Not that she wasn't doing her job. She'd arrived in the OR before the others this evening, double-checking the monitors and insuring the supply drawers were stocked.

"I'm ready to finish closing now, Katie."

Ford's warm voice—all melting Southern molasses mixed with Northern prep school polish—made her gut tighten. "Ready, Dr. Carrington," she said.

Momentarily lifting gloved hands smudged with blood, Ford scrutinized the monitors before he took a needle from Katie, leaned down and began stitching the patient, this time closing skin, not internal tissue. "Great work, everybody," he commended. "Looks like this baby's going to make it. Those monitors stable, Jerry?"

"Yeah," said a technician.

Just as another tech lowered the easy-listening country music Ford always played while he operated, he glanced up. "I appreciate your rounding up those size four clamps for me, Carrot Top. I needed them."

Katie's heartbeat quickened at the use of her nickname, and she braced herself against the unwanted feelings. "No problem," she managed to say, the end of the sentence slowing into a gait that was pure east Texas. "Dr. Nelson always grabs more of those clamps than he has a right to for OR seven. Anyway, I'm just glad this baby's going to make it."

Ford chuckled. "As slow as you talk, Katie, this boy'll be full-grown and winning rodeos before any of us leave the OR."

That got a good-natured laugh.

Katie arched a sparse red eyebrow. "Making fun of my drawl, Dr. Carrington?" He always did.

He wore a green surgical mask, and she could tell he was smiling by the way his dark brown eyes crinkled at the corners. "Is that a challenge I hear? Haven't you learned not to mess with me yet?"

"Rule number one," she returned. "Never make fun of how us Texans talk, Dr. Carrington. Those are fighting words."

"Fighting words? You think you'd win?"

"I *know*."

He chuckled. "So, you're a fighter, huh?"

"Sure am," she replied, still reminding herself that Ford Carrington didn't even know she existed outside the OR. She also knew nonmedical professionals might look askance at their casual banter and black humor, but joking relieved tension. Ford teased liberally, and Katie was the target since she could dish it out as well as take it. The repartee meant nothing special, but coming from Ford, it made her heart stutter.

Luckily, she was leaving Austin for a training program in Houston tomorrow, and she wouldn't see Ford for three months. Surely the separation would cure her hopelessly juvenile crush. "I've got two brothers, Dr. Carrington," she prompted, narrowing her green eyes wickedly, "so I didn't have much choice but to learn to fight, and fight good."

"Don't forget, I was raised in Texas, too. I might be tougher than I look."

Sometimes she kicked herself for rising to the bait—after all, he *was* Maitland Maternity's chief pediatric surgeon—but somehow, she could never stop herself. "Your Texas and my Texas are two different places," she informed him.

"That so, Carrot Top?" She watched as he surveyed his work, calmly drawing the needle through flesh. "What's my Texas?"

"Neiman Marcus, thoroughbred horses and studio-produced country music."

Only his narrowed eyes hinted at the focus he brought to his task. Unfailingly alert, they were steely and chocolate brown, flecked with gold. "And your Texas, Katie?"

"Getting grub at Pok-E-Jo's Smokehouse after a trail ride." Despite how the man set her teeth on edge without even trying, she chuckled. "If you ever want to hear *real* country music, Dr. Carrington, you just let me know."

"What's this fake country music you think I listen to?"

"Oh, you know. k.d. lang. Tanya Tucker. Dolly Parton."

He raised a lazy jet eyebrow. "What's wrong with Dolly?"

"*Old* Dolly's okay," Katie conceded. "Just not new Dolly."

"Keep it up, Katie, and I'll start thinking you're a snob."

Behind her mask, Katie's jaw dropped. "Me?"

"Yes, you."

"You're the socialite, Dr. Carrington."

"You've got me there."

Smiling, Katie glanced at the patient. The three-week-old boy on the table was named Jesse, and he hadn't had a fighting chance before this operation. Even now, it was hard to believe he'd pull through. His slight five pounds could easily be cradled in Katie's hand, and the rise and fall of the tiny, too-pale chest made her think of the delicate balance of nature in the woods she loved. Looking at the sickly child and feeling her heart pull, she thought of the tops of dandelions right before they blew away, and the fragile wings of birds, and the threads of spiderwebs. Life was so precious, and sometimes so unfairly fleeting.

Five pounds. Jesse was tiny, and yet for his mama, who was right outside the operating room, he meant the entire world. That was why, moments ago, Katie had sent a message to her, letting her know that an infected incision from a previous GI surgery had been cleaned and successfully resutured.

Katie could barely imagine the woman's stress, and yet, as many tragedies as Katie had witnessed at Maitland Maternity, she'd seen far more miracles. Glancing up, she found herself staring into eyes that made her melt. Gently, Ford probed, "You still with us, Carrot Top?"

"Sure thing." But as Ford fell to work once more, she felt strangely unsettled, as if he'd read her innermost thoughts. Deep down, she'd been wondering if she'd ever have her own little bundle of joy, her own miracle. She wanted a baby she wouldn't have to leave in the hospital nursery at the end of the day. She wanted to be the woman waiting at the curb with a newborn in her lap and a balloon tied to the arm of a wheelchair, while the man she loved brought around the car, anxious to take his family home.

Stepping slightly back from the table, Katie held her gloved hands turned upward. "Tell me when you need me again."

"Thanks, Katie."

She watched his hands, noting their size and the long, slender, mesmerizing fingers. His eyes had grown piercing in their intensity. What little of his skin was visible—mostly high, chiseled cheek-bones—was tanned the color of pecans, and through the transparent hairnet that covered a high, patrician forehead, Katie could see touchably thick, raven hair through which she'd often imagined running her fingers. When dressed in street clothes, without his scrubs, he looked more like a model than a doctor.

*Stop it!* How many times had she gazed too long into Ford Carrington's arresting midnight eyes while he closed a patient?

*Too many.*

That was why leaving Austin tomorrow was imperative. Surely, after spending three months in Houston, she'd forget about him. But so far, no matter how she fought it, he always wended his way into her thoughts. While grooming her horse, riding the mower at her papa's farm, or running to the feed store, she'd recall some moment, like a picture frozen in time: Dr. Carrington slipping from the doctors' lounge; Dr. Carrington shooting her a smile as he opened a door.

With any luck, she'd meet a man in Houston.

Already, she'd sublet her apartment, and tonight she was staying with her papa and brothers at the farm, where she still kept her horse. Houston was close enough that she could visit on weekends, but she would do her best not to. She needed the time away. Her bags were packed, her car was gassed up, and she'd convinced herself that three months without Ford would cure her of this pointless obsession.

They were night and day, after all. He was old money, and she was backwoods farm stock and proud of it. His family had come to America on the *May-*

*flower,* and pedigree was still so important to the Carringtons that Ford's mother, Yvonne, had chartered an Austin branch of the Texas Genealogical Society; his father, David, oversaw Austin's largest charity, the Carrington Foundation, which made bequests in the millions each January to health-related causes.

Society women were Ford's usual companions, and it was rumored around the hospital that he'd probably propose to Blane Gilcrest, a tall, svelte, willowy woman with straight blond hair, breasts as discreetly small as a runway model's and slender manicured fingers that she kept ringed with sparkling diamonds.

Not only was Ford practically engaged, he was seven years Katie's senior, her co-worker and mentor. Still, during tense moments in the OR, Katie knew she'd witnessed what Blane never had—the determination Ford brought to bear when saving a child's life.

Ford *had* to win against death.

What was the source of his feverish, formidable drive? she wondered. What secrets made him want suffering children to live at any cost? Why did he work so relentlessly?

Of all the surgeons at Maitland Maternity, he was the most competent, dedicated and controlled, and Katie had often seen his tough-minded tenacity win him the hearts of terrified parents, like Jesse's mama. Ever since she'd first locked eyes with him over the operating table, Katie had fallen hard.

"That's a wrap, folks," said Ford. Once he was finished, he turned, preparing to wheel out a cart of instruments.

"You don't need to get that cart," Katie protested. "It's my job."

"You think I'm afraid of a little dirty work?"

"You should be. Someone might mistake you for a nurse and make you change bedpans or worse."

"Lord knows—" Ford's dark eyes lighted on hers, sparkling in a way that seemed less than professional "—I'd swoon if I saw a bedpan. Drop into a dead faint. Now, c'mon, Carrot Top. Can you get the door for me, before you clean up our patient?"

"With pleasure. Are you going to talk to his mama?"

Ford nodded. "I'm on my way."

It was always wonderful when you could bring good news from the OR, Katie thought, wedging open the door with her hip. Simultaneously freezing and burning as Ford brushed past her, she caught a whiff of clean, male scent, noticeable among the antiseptic smells to which Katie would never become accustomed. Unexpectedly, Ford leaned closer, and she instinctively veered back, her startled eyes widening in question.

"When you're done—" his low-voiced drawl sent a shiver through her "—come over to my place, Katie. Before you leave for Houston, there are some...*things* I need to discuss with you."

"Things?"

"My address is on your desk."

She knew exactly where he lived. The house—a huge old rambling place of white-painted brick with red shutters and crisp ivy growing on trellises—was on a showy, seven-acre spread at the end of a private road. The lifestyles section of the newspaper ran articles anytime his decorator, Nan Rowe, redid so much as a bathroom. Katie's knees weakened. "Come over? But why? What—"

"Looking forward to it," Ford murmured.

Losing her usual professional composure, she half lurched after him. "Wait a minute. Ford—I mean, uh, Dr. Carrington—what *things* do you want to discuss?"

His tall, loose body merely glided over the threshold.

She stared at his back, fighting a rush of annoyance as her eyes dropped from his broad shoulders to a tight butt and long legs. Did he have any idea how much he tortured her? Or how presumptuous it was to think she'd drop everything and rush right over to his house? Not that she wouldn't go, she supposed. But what if she'd had plans?

*But you don't, do you, Katie?*

Exhaling a beleaguered sigh, she headed for the baby. *Oh, maybe Ford's interested in the training program in Houston,* she suddenly thought. *Yes, that's it. Maybe he wants to recommend it to other nurses.* Or to discuss her working with Cecil Nelson's surgical team upon her return from Houston. Yes, Ford's invitation—command, she mentally corrected, bristling again—was nothing personal. She and Ford Carrington lived worlds apart.

*But what if it was personal, Katie?* a voice niggled. Face it, she *was* leaving town tomorrow. And three months from now, when she returned, she'd be transferred to Dr. Nelson's team where her expertise was needed more. If Ford did happen to be interested in something personal...

"Hey there, Jesse," she whispered, determined to

discourage her unlikely fantasies. Her expression gentled as she stripped away the protective covering around the baby's legs. "Let's clean you up and make you presentable for your mama. She's so proud of you. We all are. You did good, kid."

Katie's eyes stung as she gazed down at the baby. For the next while, no less than if she'd been Jesse's mama, her whole world was taken up with the small, defenseless boy on the table who needed her—and the immensely satisfying knowledge that Ford Carrington had fixed things so he'd be just fine.

SECONDS AFTER FORD opened the front door, he'd realized Katie wanted to make love with him. He'd gotten home in time to change from scrubs into slacks and a lightweight knit shirt, and he'd dimmed the house lights and put on music before meeting Katie at the door with an uncorked bottle of burgundy and two full glasses.

"Welcome, Carrot Top," he'd said.

Looking a little lost on the wide porch, she'd shoved both hands into the back pockets of the skin-tight jeans she wore with cowboy boots and a University of Texas T-shirt that hugged her breasts. "Hey, Dr. Carrington," she'd returned, her deep, throaty drawl sounding as soft as velvet on the warm fall night.

Hungry, his eyes had dropped over the petite, curvy frame he rarely saw outside of scrubs. Because of where she stood, fireflies on the lawn appeared to alight in her short, tight, fiery red curls. A tiny diamond chip earring flashed from the top of her ear, where, he'd decided, the piercing had to hurt. Hospital greens definitely didn't do her justice.

"Come on in," he'd said.

Always the tease, she'd cocked her head, as if considering. "I'm unchaperoned tonight," she'd warned.

He'd glanced at her beat-up car. "True. But you did drive all the way over from the hospital."

A beatific smile had suddenly brightened her face, making the freckles scattered across her cheeks and small, straight nose jump and wiggle as she stepped across the threshold. "Don't mind if I do."

As they'd entered the dimly lit foyer, her uptilted emerald eyes had turned unmistakably smoky, and Ford suddenly realized the dark house, seductive music and heady wine had set the scene for seduction. Just as he saw stark desire spark in her eyes, the lights snapped on, illuminating a room decorated with balloons and streamers—and he found himself wishing he *had* invited Katie here to seduce her. Surprised that she might really be game for something outside the OR, Ford had mulled the possibility over as hospital staff jumped from behind furniture, shouting, "Surprise! We'll miss you, Katie! Hurry back from Houston!"

Disappointment had filled her eyes, then relief, then something that looked like sadness—but hell if Ford understood any of it. He'd been sure his teasing in the OR meant nothing to her. After work, she always vanished, almost as if she was avoiding him. He'd figured she had a hot, heavy romance. Any woman with green eyes as striking as hers probably would.

Maybe not, though. Now that the party was over and the guests had gone home, Ford was glad Katie had stayed and he could have her to himself. He leaned casually against the kitchen counter, his gaze traveling from Katie, who'd insisted on loading the dishwasher, to the living room, where party horns and paper plates still littered the tabletops. She looked up from the dishwasher. "I like those pictures you showed me in the hallway."

He glanced toward the sketches and daguerreotypes. His favorites were of Lance Carrington, who'd moved the Carrington family westward to Texas in a covered wagon, and of the Freeland branch of the family, who had gotten waylaid in what was now Kentucky. He shot her a smile. "And you thought we Carringtons were snobs."

Katie quit sorting silverware long enough to snort derisively. "Everybody in your family, including the guys on the *Mayflower,* were doctors."

"True." Chuckling, Ford rested both elbows comfortably on the counter. "But two hundred years ago, that meant selling potions from the backs of wagons and accidentally leeching people to death. Doctoring wasn't exactly a reputable profession."

When she shook her head as if to say he was impossible, light from the overhead tracks caught in her hair, turning the curls a beautiful burnished orange. His lips parted, but before he could say she possessed the most gorgeous hair in Texas, she drawled, "Are you sure you don't mind me staying to do this?"

Mind? The second Katie Topper had stepped into his foyer, he'd decided he wanted her to stay all night. "I always get post-party blues," he assured her.

Reaching into the sink, she lifted out dessert plates.

"Incorrect response, Doctor. You're supposed to say you like my company."

"What," he teased. "Fishing for compliments?"

She mock-scowled. "Maybe. What are you grinning at, anyway?"

The corners of his lips twisted into a flirtatiously devious smile. Each time she leaned to load the dishes, he got an eyeful of the best-looking backside in Austin. "Just looking at you. Scrubs and hairnets don't do you justice."

"And they supposedly enhance your appearance?"

He looked hurt. "They don't?"

"No. And if I'd known you were hosting a party in my honor," she added, shooting him an arch glance, "I would have dressed better."

"It doesn't get any better than this." His eyes drifted over the faded denim hugging her hips. "Personally, I like tight jeans on a woman."

"If you said you liked them on men, I'd start to wonder."

"Hmm. Want to turn around? Model for me?"

Smirking, she swatted her very tempting-looking rear end. "Oh, kiss my round Irish behind, Ford Carrington," she said grumpily.

"What?" Laughing, he poured himself another glass of wine and swirled it in the globe. "Be honest now. Didn't you think I asked you here to seduce you, Katie? Just for a second?"

A breathless moment passed. Recovering, she shot him a game look. "Oh, you know how we nurses are when it comes to doctors. We always hope."

He lifted his gaze, pinning hers over the rim of the glass. "Are you hoping tonight?"

"Keep dreaming," she lightly volleyed in reply.

"You're asking me to dream? I'll take that as encouragement," Ford assured, knowing she had no idea how their banter was affecting him. "There's plenty of time left for dreaming, isn't there, since the night's still young?"

Her green eyes were assessing. "Is it?"

It damn well was, and the silence that fell like a dropping curtain lasted full seconds too long. They saw each other almost daily and had teased each other mercilessly, but now they were alone in his big, empty house, with an open bottle of wine between them. After tonight she'd be gone for three months, too, plenty of time for a one-night stand to blow over.

She kept her tone deceptively conversational. "Not so young," she said, nodding toward the picture window above the sink. "See? There's already a full moon out there."

Her slow, thick accent curled into his blood, making him smile once more. In comparison, his accent was gone, educated out of him by the swanky Northeastern prep schools where his parents had sent him, and which he'd hated. She'd been right in the OR, he thought, watching her. Her Texas and his were two different places. She was a farm girl, born and bred, and even now, she talked like one. Still toying with the wine in his glass, watching the red liquid splash the sides, he drawled, "Sometimes a full moon makes all the difference in the world to a woman. Is it that way with you, Katie?"

"Only because I'm afraid of what you'll turn into."

He chuckled. "Hard to tell. A werewolf or vampire."

"Oh, no," she said darkly. "Definitely something worse."

"Definitely." Further relaxing against the counter, he wished he shared this kind of easy repartee with his crowd, instead of long, drawn-out evenings at fund-raisers, talking about stock portfolios. Breathing in the wine, he then savored the taste and immediately wished he was tasting something warmer, headier...Katie. "I'll miss you," he found himself saying, his voice catching throatily, becoming unexpectedly hoarse. "You're the best nurse we've got. And when you come back, Cecil Nelson's going to get hold of you."

As she tossed her head, her magical curls caught the light again. She laughed off the compliment. "No pun?"

Ford's eyes lingered, roving over her hair, and he took another drink of the liquor to soothe the dryness of his throat. "Pun?"

"Nelson. Getting hold of. Nelson's a wrestling hold."

Leave it to Katie to get the best of him in conversation. "No pun." And he was getting impatient with the fun and games. "When are you going to start calling me Ford, Katie?"

She grinned. "Never."

"Damn, you can be irritating," he countered with another playful smile. "C'mon, quit doing the dishes. I told you earlier, I've got a maid coming tomorrow. Have a glass of wine with me. I invited you over for your going-away party, not to clean."

Giving in, Katie dusted her hands with a dishcloth, and when her eyes found his again, she sobered. "The party was nice. Thanks…Ford."

He liked hearing her say his first name. He liked feeling those hot, searing emerald eyes on him, too. They were so sharp, so heartbreakingly green, and from working with Katie, he knew they never missed a detail. Usually, he didn't, either. How had he overlooked the soft, female intent that she was trying so hard to hide?

"I read the recommendation letter you sent to Houston," she added. "Thanks for that, too, Ford."

He'd said she was the best nurse he'd ever worked with. "It's the truth." She was wonderful. Everybody loved her. "So many people wanted to give you a send-off that only my place was big enough for the party."

She glanced around. "It *is* big."

He couldn't stop the low, suggestive and very ungentlemanly chuckle. "Size put you off?"

She sent him a droll glance. "Now, why would the size of a *house* put me off?"

Laughing, he shrugged. "I've got mixed feelings about the place myself. It was a family house, belonged to my grandfather."

The previous innuendo had brushed color across her cheeks. "The one who started the Carrington Foundation?"

The one relative that Ford felt had truly loved him. "Yeah."

Absently threading fingers through her hair, making him long to touch the springy, coiled strands, she shot another appraising look around the stainless steel kitchen. "Too big for one person," she said decisively.

"I have a lot of servants," he said defensively, though it wasn't really true.

She rolled her eyes. "Don't you get scared at night?"

His eyes locked on hers again. "Offering your company?"

"I never need company," she returned easily. "Too much Irish in my blood. I don't scare."

No, she didn't. He'd never met a nurse who was able to take so much pressure. She always hung in with him, even when it seemed too late to save a patient. Other nurses might tell him to give up, but not Katie...never Katie.

Another awkward silence fell, and the clink of glass sounded overly loud as he lifted the bottle and poured her some wine. "You've been drinking sodas all night, and I want you to try this. It's from a California vineyard owned by a friend of mine." She looked impressed, and while he wanted to impress her, he didn't like the distance it created or how put off she seemed by his money.

"Maybe too rich for my blood," she joked, still nervously running fingers through her curls. "Sure you don't have any Ripple? Night Train?"

"I'm getting no appreciation here. Most women think money's my best quality, Katie."

She surveyed him a long moment, a brief sadness touching her eyes as if she were sorry for that, then another quick smile twitched at the corners of her mouth. "Do I look like most women?"

He shook his head, his gaze slowly drifting from

hair that was like curly red ribbons to her milky, angular freckled face. "No. You're one of a kind."

Chuckling softly, she nodded toward the wine. "Okay, Dr. Carrington. You talked me into it."

"What?" he volleyed dryly. "Have you decided to stay and love me for something other than my money?"

She grinned. "Don't push your luck."

Her decision to stay awhile did crazy things to his pulse, and with blood dancing through his limbs, he said, "Care to take another walk down to the stables while you sip your wine?"

"No, but I enjoyed going earlier."

She leaned beside him at the counter, he felt as if bands of steel were tightening around his chest. He could smell soap and skin, and beneath that, something that was pure Katie. He watched as she gazed through the picture window. Earlier, he'd let two mares and a gelding out of their stalls so she could watch them run, and now the gelding bucked, playing under the moonlight. Watching the horses, she seemed to be in rapture.

"That was the nicest walk I've had for a while, Katie."

"Hard to mess up a moonlight stroll," she said, glancing from the horses and sending him a sweet sideways smile. "Mostly we gossiped."

Maitland Maternity's latest scandals had made for plenty of talk. The place hadn't been sane since the day the twenty-fifth anniversary bash was to be announced. Just before the Maitlands met the press, an unidentified baby boy, now called Cody, was found outside the hospital.

"I love gossip," Ford confessed, sipping, then lightly licking wine from his lips.

"Me, too," she said, the faint color on her face spreading downward to the smooth, unmarred skin of her neck, where he could tell her pulse was vying with his for beating too fast. Her breath suddenly caught, and the faint, involuntary sound made Ford's groin tighten, then flex.

"I love your horses," she murmured.

*Love.* Hearing the word on her lips, he flicked his gaze down the pale column of her neck again, remembering how she'd gently rubbed noses and scratched between ears until she'd found the special spot where each horse liked to be touched. There was something so genuine about Katie, so caring and unpretentious that she'd stolen his breath. He edged closer. "I can tell you like them."

"They're beautiful, Ford."

When she glanced up, he could swear the clear emerald slits of her eyes held invitation. At least, Ford hoped he wasn't misreading the situation. Risking it, he murmured, "You're beautiful, Katie." Very slowly, his eyes fixed intently on hers, he pushed aside his wineglass.

He could see her fingers tremble as she pushed her glass away, too. When her hand stilled, resting on the base, he knew she wasn't steadying the glass but herself. Her voice held a tremor. "Maybe I'd better go home now, Dr. Carrington."

"Ford," he corrected huskily, catching her hand. "And I know you don't want to leave, Katie." With the words, his chest squeezed out the rest of his breath. "Stay. Let me give you the proper send-off."

Seeing her gemstone eyes smolder with want, he threaded their fingers, bringing her hand to his chest. His response was amazing. He shuddered, and as his nipple beaded beneath her fingertips, he could barely process what was happening. Why hadn't he guessed that, outside the OR, Katie Topper's touch would shoot through him like wild volts of electricity? Why hadn't he guessed she'd feel the same?

Katie sounded shaky. "Proper send-off?"

"Okay," he admitted. "Not so proper." No, what he had in mind wasn't proper at all. Gently cupping her neck, he tilted back her head and glided his fingers into the flaming red curls he'd longed to touch all night. "Your hair's soft as silk, Katie," he murmured, rubbing strands between his fingertips. Bending, he released a shuddering sigh and pressed an unbroken strand of wet kisses from her ear to her collarbone, the sugar-salt flavor of her skin making his pulse fracture.

She melted. There was no other word for it. He felt the limbs of her petite body loosen and stretch and felt heat rise from her as if she were a burning taper. Groaning, he wrapped an arm tightly around her back, his groin thickening, becoming almost painful. "I've been fighting this all night," he confessed, gasping as her hipbone ground against him. Ever so slowly, he stroked the space behind her ear with his tongue.

"We work together, Ford," she whispered. "We're two completely different people...."

"Did you hear me asking for a lifetime, Katie?" Ford half coaxed, half chided, his palms traveling down her back, molding the firm backside snuggled beneath tight jeans, while his five o'clock shadow roughened the creamy skin of her neck. "This is good old-fashioned lust," he assured hoarsely, "nothing more." Attempting to ignore how her denials prickled his male vanity, demanding he claim her, he kissed her velvet skin, deciding that days from now, when she was in Houston, she'd remember every minute of what he was about to do to her. "I'm too old for you, Katie," he repeated, desire making the words sound strained. "And I'm someone you work with. I've got a whole other lifestyle. But I'm a confirmed bachelor, too. At thirty-six, I know exactly what I want."

Breathless, Katie whispered, "You do, Ford?"

"Yeah." Releasing a low moan, he kissed his way up her neck, along her jaw, around her chin. "Yeah. I know exactly what I want. You, Katie." His mouth covered hers, and as he registered the soft pliancy of her wanting lips, an unforgettable aching claimed him. Her taste—all dark wine and mint toothpaste and pent-up longing—sent luscious shivers rippling through him. Harder, his hungry mouth swooped and crushed. No, he wouldn't rest until Katie Topper was naked and beneath him.

Already, he was imagining lifting off her T-shirt, pushing back her bra, freeing her breasts. Already, as he deeply, silkily thrust his tongue between her lips, he was admitting this woman could probably make him lose his mind. Beneath her shirt, the tips of her breasts had pebbled. When he became aware of the roughened nubs brushing his chest, a streak of lightning shot to his groin. "One night." Sharply, he pulled in a breath of her. "I don't want anything more than that, Katie."

"No," she agreed raggedly. "I don't, either."

Leaning back just a fraction, he swept a ravenous gaze from her well-kissed, wine-red lips to the red mark he'd left on her perfect neck. Further down, seeing the tight buds he intended to taste showing through her top, he thought he'd explode. Tightening his fingers through hers, he hoarsely said, "Come with me."

"Where?"

"To my bed, Katie."

# CHAPTER TWO

*Three months later*

"WE DISCUSSED moving Katie to my team ages ago." Dr. Cecil Nelson, seated on a bench in the doctors' shower room, turned away from the lockers, toward Ford and lifted a small, red-and-green gift-wrapped package, weighing it so carefully in his hand that it could have been a gold nugget on the scales of justice. After a lengthy moment's consideration, he set it aside. "Ford," he continued, "what's gotten into you?"

"Be kind, Cecil. 'Tis the season."

Hardly looking ready to spread donated gifts and good cheer throughout the hospital, Cecil offered a grumpy "Humph," shot Ford a surly look, then pinched a lint speck from the Santa costume he was about to put on. Staring at Cecil's beefy hand, Ford shook his head, and Cecil suddenly laughed, holding the hand up for inspection. "People swore I'd never make it through med school."

"You showed them."

"Ay-yeah, young man," Cecil agreed, his slow drawl elongating vowels and slurring consonants. "These hands might look more suited to manual labor than precision surgery, but I graduated top of the class. Showed them, indeed. Was born poorer than a son of a gun, too.'' White-haired and burly, Cecil was just a year from retirement, and being the sort of wily Southern doctor who was far smarter than his manner of speech might indicate, and who always meandered before making his point, he only now added, ''I look more like Santa than a cardiac specialist, too, Ford, but when I get a gift as good as Katie Topper, I don't give her away. That little spitfire's joining my team when she gets back to town.''

''Little spitfire,'' Ford repeated with a chuckle. ''If she heard you call her that, she'd serve you up on a platter.''

Cecil's bushy white eyebrows drew together. ''What's wrong with little spitfire?''

''It's right up there with little lady, Cecil. You're an educated man, you ought to know better.''

Cecil's lips twitched. ''Feel free to sue me. I'm both Texan and male, and if anybody thinks I can still disturb a young nurse as pretty as Katie Topper at the ripe old age of sixty-four, I'd be more than flattered. Anyway, the point is that she's my favorite nurse.''

''She's everybody's favorite nurse.''

''Maybe, but she's mine when she gets back. I need her.''

''Not like I do.''

''What do you need her for?''

*Plenty.* Ford needed her the way a man needed a woman. Nearly three months had passed, but his mind drifted to her at the strangest times. At night he'd find himself painfully aroused, the sheets damp and twisted on the floor, his head full of Katie's sweet moans. Before that night, Ford had accustomed himself to cool, distant women with too much eastern education and too little down-home desire. Women who, if the truth be told, had eyes that generally strayed to one place—a man's wallet—and who viewed sex as an inconvenient requirement that came with marrying the right kind of man. Women like Blane Gilcrest, who had been trying—and failing— to arouse Ford's interest ever since her daddy, the attorney for the Carrington Foundation, had gotten close to Ford's father. Lanky and blond, Blane prided herself on being the kind of woman Ford needed, but he knew her beauty only went skin deep. She was all smooth polish, transparent as glass. Totally unlike Katie.

Katie had been glorious in her passion, her milk-pale silken skin damp and on fire, creamy in places most men didn't see, as mouthwateringly sweet as honeysuckle where her freckles ended and as fresh as dew where sun and skin never met. Her plump pink mouth, always so sassy, had slackened with release, and her upturned green eyes, always so sharp, had glazed like boiling sugar. She'd given as good as she got, just as she did in the OR, and she'd turned Ford on as he'd never been before. Just as she'd tested his horses that night in the stables, finding their weakest spots, she'd tested him and discovered secrets no other woman had ever bothered looking for. It wasn't because Katie was so experienced, either, but because she made love the way a woman should, with her heart.

"So, what do you say, Ford?"

"What, Cecil?"

Cecil squinted, then suddenly slapped his thigh and

loosed a belly laugh. "Hope you're done for the day."

"All I've got left is the insertion of a feed tube."

"Good. 'Cause you're definitely not playing with a full deck at the moment. While you were busy thinking, I said maybe Katie can shift back in another few months, but I need her now. About a week ago, when she called, I could tell she's done great things in Houston. Fact is, I think that little spitfire knows more about the human heart than I do at this point, and since my team covers heart and lungs, we want to see what she learned. Some of the other nurses are considering enrolling in that Houston program, too."

Ford's mind, usually as sharp as spurs, hadn't quite caught up. "You talked to her?"

Cecil nodded. "She called last week. They loved her there, even offered her a job. Scared me, since we need her."

Katie had phoned Cecil? She was thinking of taking a job in Houston? Ford had considered calling her for months, but every time he picked up the phone, he'd visualize her lying across his bed—short-winded, her chest heaving and lamplight from his upstairs hallway shooting streaks of gold through her tight red curls. He wished that he hadn't, in the last breathless minute before he'd removed her clothes, reiterated the reasons they wouldn't make a good couple—that he was too rich, too much older than she was, too caught up in a world unlike her own. At the time, he'd meant it. Women like Blane, not Katie, peopled his life.

But the body had a mind of its own, and now he'd crawl right out of his skin if he didn't make love to her again. Unfortunately, after sex that had taken the back of his head clear off, he'd awakened to find her gone—as if she couldn't leave fast enough. No note. No panties he might keep in his drawer to remember her by. Nothing.

Because he was a gentleman—at least sometimes— for three months, he'd left the ball in Katie's court. Now he'd started thinking that if she worked with him in the OR again, she might decide to date him. Maybe they could just start off slow and easy. Grab a bite to eat. See a movie. See what happened.

"She didn't take the job, right?" Ford asked casually.

"I assume she didn't. She would have said otherwise."

Ford's mind turned over, playing the options. "But there's a chance she'll move to Houston?"

Cecil's blue eyes were as intrusive as scalpels, and his powerful shoulders suddenly shook with merriment. "About *five minutes ago* I said I wasn't positive, Ford. But I guess you quit listening."

"When did she call?"

"Last week. Keep it up and I'll think you want to move Katie to your team for personal reasons."

"Oh, you're swift, Cecil," Ford said. "You caught me."

Cecil laughed. "You're crazy."

Ford thought about the night they'd spent together. It *had* been crazy. Hot, sweaty and wild. They'd shared the kind of sex people only dreamed about.

"I'd forget about her if I was you, Ford."

Since there'd be no forgetting that night, Ford decided the older surgeon was starting to get on his nerves. "Why?"

"Your lives couldn't be more different. You've got a fancy East-coast education, money, family, power. If you want the best table in Austin, any maître d' will move the governor of the state to give it to you. But Katie Topper?" Cecil's chuckles got the best of Ford, darkening his mood, mostly because he knew what the elderly man was thinking: for once, Ford Carrington, who'd been born chewing a silver spoon, was going to have trouble getting something he wanted.

But there was a lot Cecil didn't know.

Like most men who'd pulled themselves up by the bootstraps, Cecil couldn't imagine the wealthy having any hardships. He'd never guess what it had been like for Ford—a lone child in a big house who, at the age of ten, had felt blamed for his little brother's death. Cecil would never guess how, despite his professed hatred for medicine, Ford had become a surgeon to win family approval that never came, or that to this day, the cold withdrawal of parents for whom he professed not to care had left a core of anger burning in Ford, just as strongly as the desire to find love. Inside him was an empty hole that no one had ever really filled. But just for a second, on a night three months ago, he'd felt satisfied, maybe even loved. No woman had ever touched him the way Katie had, which was why he was still single at thirty-six.

No, a man like Cecil wouldn't understand. Maybe Katie Topper wouldn't, either. Ford hadn't forgotten how her eyes had assessed his house, and while he'd sensed her ability to love a man not for what he did or owned but for who he really was, Ford knew she was put off by wealth. He'd noted it in the OR, when they teased each other. Like Cecil, she seemed to think that silver spoons bought the end of trouble. But the truth was, money always had a price.

Cecil was still laughing. "Sorry, Ford, but even if Katie had been secretly in love with you for years, you'd never get hold of an Irish spitfire like that without a fight."

"Fine by me." Ford smiled easily. "You know I live for the challenge." Difference was, where Katie would come out swinging, Ford was the type to apply slow, silent pressure. He'd win, too. Cecil was right. The all-powerful Carringtons had everything at their command, including wealth, charm, connections and good looks.

Ford Carrington had everything but Katie.

And while he'd probably never be the marrying kind, he'd decided months ago that she was coming back to his bed.

THE PHONE RANG, and for a missed heartbeat, she was sure the caller was Ford. "If it is, don't be a wuss, Katie Topper!" she coached nervously, pacing around her apartment. "Just tell him the truth, hear what he says, and if he blows his stack, calmly tell him you'll think things over and get right back to him."

Slipping an anxious hand over her belly, she felt her heart pull with a bittersweet mix of excitement, joy and worry for which there was no name in the English language. Then, startled into action, she began quickly tossing aside empty boxes and lifting couch cushions, muttering, "C'mon, where are you, phone?"

Before she'd left for Houston, she had sublet the apartment furnished but had packed her breakables, and since she'd spent Christmas at her papa's farm, she'd only now gotten around to unpacking. Not the most thrilling New Year's Eve she'd ever spent, she thought, wishing her brothers hadn't had dates and that her papa hadn't left town for a few weeks, as he often did, to do a contracting job in Dallas. Of course Katie had lived through worse. *Yeah, like the past three months when you didn't so much as see Ford Carrington.*

It took six rings to unbury the phone and another to take a very deep breath just in case it was Ford. Why Katie bothered, she didn't know. It had been a one-night stand, pure and simple. No man could have been clearer about wanting only sex. Wham, bam, thank you, ma'am. Trouble was, every blessed second had been pure, delicious fantasy, as if Ford Carrington had looked into her mind and then done everything she'd imagined. It had been three o'clock before common sense and pride kicked in and Katie bolted, heading to the farmhouse and sneaking into bed. How could she have given herself so brazenly to a man who so clearly didn't want more from her? Sure, she'd *said* she didn't want a relationship, but she'd been lying.

"And you still are, at least by omission," she snapped as she punched the talk button, still wondering what she'd say if it *was* him. Just a quick, *Hi there, Ford. I'm pregnant.* Or, *Remember how I said I liked dining at Pok-E-Jo's? Well, it's all ice cream and pickles now, cowboy.* Maybe she should have taken the job in Houston and solved the problem by simply vanishing. "Happy New Year," she found herself saying, nervously tapping her bare foot on the wood floor. "So far, it's shaping up to be a doozy. Katie speaking."

"I hope you don't have plans tonight, sweetheart."

Realizing how tightly she was clutching the phone, Katie relaxed. A relieved sigh whooshed from her chest. "Sue? Is that you?"

"Yes, aren't you lucky," the nursing coordinator from Maitland Maternity said in a rush. "It's me. And I'm majorly glad you're home. You're not due at work for a couple of weeks—I know that—but I gave as many people as possible the night off since it's New Year's Eve, and now we've got an emergency. We need another nurse and a surgeon and—"

She fought it, but the name escaped. "Ford?"

"Dr. Carrington's cohosting a party at Blane Gilcrest's. You know, that socialite he dates who's always in the papers? She's got that mansion on Lakeview? Anyway, I'm looking for Cecil Nelson. He's on call."

Katie barely heard. Jealousy had come to her in a quick, unwanted mental flash of Ford dancing with Blane under soft, fuzzy lights. Or whatever. Who knew what wealthy people did on New Year's?

Katie's eyes slid to the TV, where, just an hour shy of midnight, the ball was dropping on Times Square, and she calmly reminded herself she had no right to the murderous feelings coursing through her. What happened between her and Ford, while magical for her, was a one-time thing. That was the deal.

Of course there was a small hitch now.

Which meant she'd somehow have to look straight into the dark irresistible eyes that had drunk in her naked body and forget the moment she'd conceived. She felt herself flush as she recalled the coarse hair of Ford's legs and chest, how she'd soared when his mouth locked over her breasts and how she'd whimpered when his fingers curled possessively between her thighs. Katie exhaled a shudder.

She'd been a fool to think making love with Ford would get him out of her system, or that she could deny her feelings and chalk the night up to an excess of the fancy wine from his friend's vineyard. If she was honest about it, she'd only had one sip, anyway.

Even if Ford expressed interest now—which he wouldn't—she couldn't sleep with him again, not ever. He was high-society Austin, and she was a farm girl. He'd said he wanted sex, not a relationship, and Katie had too much self-respect to let herself be accused of trying to trap a rich man with a pregnancy.

"Can you get over here?" Sue was saying. "I'll keep looking for Dr. Nelson. But we've got a week-old girl in trouble. We thought we could wait until tomorrow to correct a blockage in her esophagus—"

"On my way." Katie switched off the phone, shoved her feet into cowboy boots and grabbed her keys. She flicked off the TV, then ran for the car, realizing when the sharp January night air chilled her that she'd forgotten a coat. Not that she'd go back. A baby was in trouble.

Later, she'd think about the new life inside her and whether she should have contacted Ford before now. She was a nurse and prided herself on practicality;

nevertheless, for two months she'd convinced herself her missed periods were due to the temporary move to Houston. Just female pheromones adjusting to her new coworkers, she'd kept thinking…until she'd administered the pregnancy test that proved she was pregnant and in plain, old-fashioned denial. She simply didn't understand how it happened. They'd used condoms. "Plural," she whispered with a sigh.

At first, the knowledge of her pregnancy burned inside her, but she'd only broken down once, confiding in her friend Hope Logan without identifying the father. Hope would be flabbergasted if she knew. But Katie wanted this baby desperately, though she had no illusions of receiving help from Ford. He was thirty-six and a confirmed bachelor by his own admission. Not even the polished social butterflies who flocked around him had caught his interest, so Katie figured she didn't have a prayer.

"How am I going to tell him?" she muttered, stomping her foot and inadvertently making the car lunge forward. "Well, whatever he says, I'll take him on."

Her papa, too. She couldn't tell him before Ford, but she was worried about how he'd react. Jack Topper was sternly religious, yes, but he was a contractor and old-fashioned Texas farmer, too, which meant he'd either head for the prayer rail at New Flock Baptist or grab the first handy rifle, point it at Ford and try to force him to marry her. Telling Jack it was the twenty-first century and that people no longer solved things with double-barreled blue steel wouldn't deter him one bit, either.

"Concentrate, Katie," she whispered as she sped

toward Maitland Maternity. "And thank fate for small favors." At least she'd probably be working with Cecil Nelson tonight, which meant she'd been granted another reprieve, however brief, before she told Ford Carrington she was pregnant with their baby.

SHE'S PREGNANT.

It was an instinctive, gut reaction, entirely unfounded but born of years spent working around pregnant women. That, and remembering the broken condom he hadn't told Katie about. Only years of medical experience allowed Ford to separate the personal and professional and throw every ounce of his energy into fixing up a newborn. "Pressure?"

"Stable," Katie said.

"Oxygen? Saline? Drips?"

She read off strings of numbers.

The professional tone left Ford feeling faintly murderous, even though he knew she, too, needed to dissociate from her emotions in order to get this job done; without that skill, people could never accomplish tasks that, anywhere outside an OR, would be considered barbaric. What was barbaric was Blane's New Year's party, Ford thought. Beach theme. Drinks with umbrellas. Mascot in diapers. He'd felt as if he was still a frat boy, back in college, and he couldn't have been more relieved when the hospital called, saying they were still looking for Cecil.

Ford glanced at Katie again. Surely, his initial impression that she was pregnant was unfounded, but in the heartbeat before she'd pulled on her mask, he'd noted the deepening skin color and rounding of her face. Lord, was wishful thinking making him imagine she'd come back from Houston, her belly filling with their child? Always emotionally unattached, his only model the family in which he'd grown up, he'd never considered having a baby. But with a woman like Katie, could things be different?

Her eyes were still evading his, settling everywhere else in the crowded room full of milling nurses and technicians, making his mind run wild. Didn't seeing him for the first time in three months affect her at all? He'd expected at least a glimmer of awareness, a re-kindled spark. Was she embarrassed, since they'd been in his bed the last time they'd spoken?

"Scalpel."

Their fingertips met. Even through gloves, he felt her quickening pulse, the sudden, sensual tremor of her skin. Fearing she might not feel it, too, he silently cursed her for making him want her so much. He forced himself to look away and continue working, but it was hard to concentrate. He kept seeing the wrecked living room and the faint lip-gloss smudge on a wineglass, both of which had told him the night with her hadn't been his imagination. Why had she left him nothing? Not even a lipsticked message on a mirror. Or a scribbled note in a sport coat pocket for him to find weeks later.

He focused, needing to connect two blocked ends of a malformed esophagus. Simple but delicate, the operation served as a reminder of how much people took for granted. Things like tasting and swallowing nourishment, or pulling life's sweetest scents all the way down into your lungs. That one night, Katie had been exactly like this, simple but delicate. And by damn, he was getting her back into his bed, one way or the other.

Only when he finished the last stitch did he look at her again. "When you're done, can I speak with you outside?"

Her green eyes looked worried. "In the hallway?"

He figured whatever they had to say to each other didn't belong to the gossip mill of Maitland Maternity. "No. Outside. The parking lot."

FORD LEANED against the driver's door of Katie's car just in case she decided to hop in, speed off and evade him, the way she used to after work. Damn it, was he simply acting like a possessive, rejected fool? The idea soured his mood. As he stared toward the OR doors, waiting for her, he realized he didn't take kindly to being thrown off stride. That was the good thing about women like Blane. He knew how to handle them. He glanced around. Katie had parked under a streetlight, but otherwise, the lot was dark and empty, and the night was cold, even for December in Austin.

"January," he corrected, since the clock had ticked over into the new year while he and Katie were working. The operation had gone well, so where was she? Changing into party clothes, as he had? Had she been celebrating the new year with a lover? The father of the baby? Maybe it wasn't his....

"She's not pregnant," he muttered in angry exasperation, wishing his mind would let go of the ludicrous thought.

Unfair as it was, he felt relieved to see her come outside wearing hospital greens and carrying folded jeans, which probably meant she hadn't been any-where. Not wanting to appear anxious, he kept lean-ing against the car, watching her, listening to the hard, solid connection of her boot heels on the pavement until she stopped in front of him. Somehow, he ex-pected three months to have changed her, but she was the same familiar Katie. His eyes drifted hungrily over red coils of hair that had grown a fraction, and he recalled trailing fingers down the vibrant strands to smooth, now winter-pale cheeks, and how he'd played connect-the-dots with the freckles on her shoulders.

Anxiously, she cleared her throat. "Uh…hi, Dr. Carrington."

She probably hadn't planned that opening line, any more than he planned the traitorous tightening of his body when the soft Texas slur of her words churned his blood into a wild current. *Hi, Dr. Carrington.* It seemed a damn funny thing to say, since the last words she'd said to him were, *Please, Ford, can't we sleep like this?* She'd meant with their naked bodies still hot, damp and joined. He'd smiled, informing her that sleep wasn't in her future. And it hadn't been.

"Told you I'd be waiting, Katie." Before she could answer, he added, "And I really think you should call me Ford."

"I guess I should," she returned, swallowing hard. "Yes…I really guess so." Her bright green eyes skated to where he was leaning against the car, and she peered at him through a fringe of red eyelashes. "I said I'd meet you. I wasn't going anywhere, you know."

Maybe not, but she sounded as if she wished she

were, something that further darkened Ford's disposition. Hadn't she had the slightest interest in seeing him again? "Did I say you were leaving? Anyway, where's your coat?"

She dropped her stacked clothes on the hood. "Sue said it was an emergency, so I just ran out the door." Her eyes flicked over his tux and gray wool overcoat. "But I take it you were ringing in the New Year somewhere special?" Leaving him to wonder if she was jealous, she quickly added, "Sue assured me she was looking for Dr. Nelson."

Assured? Ford guessed that meant Katie no longer wanted to work with him. "Well, Sue got me." And Katie was biding time, alluding to the party at Blane's, where, Ford didn't exactly feel inclined to tell her, he'd been bored out of his mind. Shrugging from the topcoat, he said, "Here."

Katie tossed her head, and nothing more than the mild reminder of her fiery independence threatened to set him off. Watching her crisp curls glint under the lamplight seemed such a travesty, too, when he wanted to feel them wrapping around his fingertips like springs of raw red silk.

"Thanks, but I don't need a coat."

"Yes, you do."

"Really." She shivered. "I'm fine."

"Right." The ungiving cotton of the short-sleeved greens tightly hugged her breasts, making plainly visible what the chill air was doing to her. He glanced away, but not before getting a good look at how she was affected. He waved the coat at her. "Katie. C'mon. Take it." If she didn't and he took another good look at her, he might do something he'd regret.

"I said I don't need it."

The words were out before he could stop them. "No," he drawled coolly. "I guess proud Katie Topper doesn't need a thing." He hardly knew where the words came from, but she sure hadn't given their night together any thought.

She looked startled. "What's that supposed to mean?"

"Nothing," he muttered.

But when she snagged the coat from the crook of his finger, swirled it around her shoulders and hugged it to her belly, Ford had another gut feeling his deepest suspicions weren't unfounded. He glanced from the hem, which brushed her ankles, to the shoulder seams halfway down her arms. Even though the ill fit made her look petite and feminine as hell, Ford swore to himself that he wouldn't react. Then he went for broke. "I know this sounds crazy, Katie, but are you pregnant or something?"

She gasped, then stomped her foot on the pavement, fisting her hands. "I knew you'd guessed, Ford! Why didn't you just say so? Yes. Yes, it is true, Ford. I'm pregnant! I'm pregnant!"

The sudden outburst, so like Katie, ended as abruptly as it began, leaving noticeable silence in its wake. The hospital was hushed, and the winter night too cold for the insects whose wings usually hummed under the street lamps. When Ford drew air into his lungs again, the inhalation seemed to whisper as if telling a secret. He started to suggest they get in her car so they could run the heater while they talked, but he couldn't risk being in such a small, enclosed space with her. In close proximity, he'd either throttle her or do what he shouldn't allow himself to do before this was settled—make love to her.

*A baby.* He'd handled so many, but was the woman in front of him really carrying his? He could so easily imagine how Katie would look, full with his flesh, his blood. The thought startled him. He didn't know exactly when, couldn't pinpoint the moment, but he'd given up thinking about becoming a father. He was thirty-six and single, too damn old. He knew he couldn't settle down with any of the women he'd known. He didn't much like them. But now...

She'd paled, her translucent skin turning the color of paper. "Uh...how did you guess?"

Images were still filling his mind, of watching her belly becoming rounder, of holding the baby in his hands. "I'm surrounded by pregnant women sixty hours a week, Katie, just as you are." And yet it was more than that, as if he were simply in tune with Katie.

She nodded, suddenly looking small and strangely miserable, nearly swallowed up by his coat, and yet as she spoke, she thrust her chin upward in an imperious way he found truly annoying under the circumstances. "I...I'm sorry. I should have called."

No kidding. "If you're trying to piss me off by saying that, Katie," he warned, "you're doing a fine job. You're sure it's mine?"

As the remaining color drained from her face, making the freckles on her nose more visible, he realized he didn't feel as guilty as he should have about wounding her pride, not when she hadn't even bothered to call him. Her voice was a near whisper. "Of course it is, Ford."

"No man in Houston?"

She looked totally taken aback. "No."

"No man *here?*"

Her eyes narrowed, glittering. "No!"

He forced himself not to acknowledge his relief. "But I didn't rate a phone call?"

"I'm here, aren't I?"

"Only because you were called in for an emergency." He couldn't help but point it out, barely able to believe her silence or the fact that he was going to be a father. "For all I know, you were considering taking that job in Houston. Cecil said they offered you one. Maybe you're still planning to go back?"

"No. I'm staying." She stared at him a second. "At least I think so."

As if he'd force her to leave. "Were you going to tell me?"

Her lips parted with shock. "What do you think?"

"I don't know, that's why I'm asking."

"Yes."

A stranger seemed to get hold of him, one with less pride than Ford usually possessed. Or more anger. "But you *didn't* tell me, did you, Katie?"

"You're not making this easy, Ford."

"I don't intend to."

"I was nervous," she explained, and as she stepped defensively back, he reached out, wrapped a hand around her upper arm and drew her toward him. Too late, he realized he'd brought her just inches away. For an instant, Ford almost forgot the conversation. It took everything he had not to kiss her, but he could never allow himself the pleasure, not when she hadn't even called him. She wanted him to kiss her, though.

That was the hell of it. Her mouth puckered. Her lips parted. And as pleased as he was to see desire spark in those come-hither green eyes, it threatened to gentle his emotions, so he loosened his hold.

She wrenched away, rubbing her upper arm as if he'd done real damage, which he hadn't. "Never grab me like that."

"I'll never touch you again. I promise."

He immediately wished he hadn't spoken. Not that it mattered. Her eyes said she knew it was a lie. "I was going to call you from Houston," she told him. "But this seemed like news I should deliver face to face. And the weekends I did drop by the hospital, you were off."

"Yeah," he muttered. "I guess you made sure of that. But you could have driven to my place." He glanced away, fighting emotions he couldn't even begin to untangle. They'd been together only one night, he'd desperately wanted her back in his bed for months, but now they'd be tied together for life. Life was a long time. Even with a woman whose body he craved as much as Katie's. "When did you find out?"

"I guessed weeks ago, but I just kept thinking…."

He thrust a hand angrily through his thick dark hair, rumpling it. "Thinking you weren't pregnant?" Damn it, didn't she mean hoping she wasn't?

When she nodded, he tried not to react, but he was remembering their first kiss in his kitchen, the party plates and streamers still in the next room. After all the time they'd worked together, how could he have so completely misjudged her? Hadn't she wanted this baby? Even for an instant?

Her voice was stern. "I'm keeping it, Ford."

Relief flooded him, but the way she'd said it...
"You'd consider something else?" He knew she'd
never guess at the anger rushing through his veins,
but he couldn't stop the fingers that tightened over
hers. Then he suddenly lost it. A hand was in her hair,
skimming the waves, tightening on her scalp and de-
fying her by pulling her to him again. His voice was
raspy. "Of course you're keeping this baby, Katie."

Her eyes, a fraction away, blinked rapidly, almost
as if she was fighting tears. "I am?" The voice was
faint, curious. "I thought you might have a problem
with this...uh, Ford."

"Hell, yes, I have a problem with this. I'm in
shock. This is totally out of the blue. But I save lives,
Katie. I don't take them. Who do you think I am,
anyway?"

"That's the point, isn't it?" she returned, backing
nervously away, cuddling his coat more tightly
around her. "We've worked together a long time,
Ford, but we don't even know each other, not really."

*Well enough to make a baby.* "Maybe not. But it
looks like we're going to." His eyes lowered to her
lips, and he realized that three months had done nothing to erase the memory of their taste. Soft, plump
and lightly glossed, he knew them well. He'd suckled
and bitten and nipped, and they'd held fast, kissing
him back.

The huskiness of her low voice brought him to his
senses. "You don't have to be involved, Ford."

Usually he was expert at pushing people away.
Yes, Ford Carrington had turned that into a fine art.
"Keep dreaming, Katie," he found himself saying,

"I'm going to be involved. Oh, I understand. Before you left, you said you didn't want me in your life—"

"Whoa!" she burst out. "You said you didn't want a relationship. It was mutual."

"We agree on that, anyway—" His barely perceptible drawl grew thicker and more pronounced. "It was very definitely mutual, Katie." As his eyes traced her lips, there was no denying he wanted her sexually. But he needed to think about this. A baby? He'd avoided this situation for years. Could he give a child what it needed?

"Ford—" She was trying to stay calm. "I don't think you understand. We come from completely different backgrounds. My papa's really religious, and now I've got to tell him I'm having a baby when I'm not even married. He's not the kind of man who'll be able to accept that I..."

"Slept around?"

"It's not like I do it all the time! This wasn't supposed to happen! We used protection!"

"The condom broke."

She stared at him a long moment, her breath the only thing that moved, clouding on the night air. Nervously, she licked her lips, and he could see her throat working as she swallowed, the wildly beating pulse at her neck giving away her emotions. Finally, she whispered, "You didn't tell me?"

He blew out a sigh. "I didn't want to worry you."

"You didn't want to worry me?" she echoed.

She knew the odds. "The chance of this happening is next to nil." She hugged the coat even more tightly around her and shifted her weight as if she was getting colder. "What are we going to do, Ford?"

Hell if he knew. He shook his head. He'd fantasized about her coming back from Houston, then to his house with a bottle of burgundy and an invitation to bed. Now the vision included having a newborn curled against his chest. He glanced away, the globe of a streetlight capturing his attention, then some tree branches swaying in the wind. Frowning, he carefully considered all the options, then simply said what he'd sworn he never would. "Marry me."

Katie was stunned into silence, then from between gritted teeth, she suddenly growled, "You can kiss my round Irish behind, Ford Carrington!"

His jaw slackened. He stared at her. Hadn't he just offered the best possible solution? Shouldn't a woman in her shoes want a husband right now? He'd never imagined proposing marriage, much less getting rebuffed. He was so taken aback, he couldn't help but mutter, "I believe I did."

Katie's lips parted in shock. "Did what?"

"Kissed your round Irish behind," he reminded her gruffly, edging closer. "Nearly three months ago. Gave you a smart little nip on the left cheek from what I recall, Carrot Top."

As cold as the air was, Ford figured her response—a sharp, audible inhalation—had to hurt her lungs. "Uh, that was months ago, and we've got other things to talk about now, Ford."

*No kidding.*

"I figure it might be best if I take another job," she continued quickly, clasping her hands nervously, as if aware this wasn't going very well. "At Texas General. Or in Houston. As Cecil told you, they offered me a job, but I wanted to come home...."

Maybe she simply hadn't heard him. "I said, marry me, Katie."

Angry tears filled her eyes, and even though he knew the barely concealed emotion was directed at him—or maybe because it was—he wanted to wrap her in his arms. The urge to kiss her was sudden, visceral. He wanted to lower his mouth to hers, not letting her breathe until all that anger turned to passion.

"Marry you?" she said in a furious tone. "Why? Because you're afraid I won't give you any rights to your baby otherwise? Is that it, Ford? You don't trust me?"

"I admit," he couldn't help but say, "that after all the time we've worked together, Katie, I wouldn't have suspected you could be pregnant with my child without telling me."

"I've only known myself for a few weeks," she said defensively. "And if you want to be involved, you can."

He released a frustrated sigh. "If? You're talking about my child here, Katie. Marry me."

"Why?" she countered again. "Are you afraid of how people will react?" Suddenly, she nodded. "Oh, I see. Having a baby out of wedlock would be a strike against the Carrington family name."

"Yes, it would," he agreed. Not that he cared. "And it sounds as if it would be a strike against the Topper name, too."

"We Toppers might not have much materially, but we have values, Ford. Marriage means something to me!"

He'd about had it. "And it doesn't to me?"

"Your crowd marries for money and status," she returned heatedly.

That much was true. "So?"

"So, I can't talk about marriage in the way you do."

"The way I do?"

"Yeah, in that calm, cool, collected voice, like it doesn't mean anything more than sharing a house with a woman who keeps her own friends and bedroom."

"I asked you to marry me, Katie," he retorted. "I don't recall saying anything about separate bedrooms."

She gaped at him. "You're not in love with me, Ford!"

He wasn't even sure what love was. "No, I'm not."

She pressed a hand to her forehead. "Look, this conversation is getting too personal."

"Marriage is personal, Katie." So was the energy current flowing between them as fast as a flooding river. Ford had no idea where it was taking them, only that the ride would be memorable.

"Marriage and childbirth are sacred to me, Ford," she managed to say. "So is extended family. My mama died when I was kid, but I remember how it was with her, how close we were. My family's still close. Family's the most important thing in the world to me." Color had flooded her cheeks. "I..." She paused, tightening her clasped hands. "Look, you're not in love with me, so why are you doing this?"

He was still thinking about the tensions in his family, and he had to admit she was right. Marriages in his crowd were often cold. People made convenient, public matches, then had private affairs for other needs. But Katie was a warm woman. She needed more. She needed a loving man in her bed every night. "There's more to the proposition," he said.

She looked wary. "Really?"

"Really." In a voice gone soft with seduction, he murmured, "There's ten million dollars involved, Katie."

She blinked, but to his surprise and her credit, she didn't miss a beat. "You say that like you expect me to sell my soul to the devil, Ford Carrington."

He smiled. "Not to the devil, Katie. To me."

She looked as curious as she was cautious, and he suddenly wondered if he'd found a woman who really would marry only for love. "Hmm," she said. "You and the devil. Why do I get the impression that at the moment there's not much of a difference between the two?"

"Because there isn't." Now that he had her attention, he proceeded to explain the stipulation in his grandfather's will. "I've always said I'm a committed bachelor, and my grandfather was worried I wouldn't leave any Carrington heirs, so as an incentive, the next blood Carrington born gets a big chunk of change. Ten million. It comes out of the funds for the Carrington Foundation, which he started before he died." So what if he'd also been lusting for Katie Topper? he thought. So what if having this baby excited him more than he wanted to admit? "It's only practical. Think hard before you answer me, Katie."

Her expression held equal parts frank curiosity and outraged fury. "And to think I've admired you," she finally said stiffly. Raising her voice, she added, "*Think?* Oh, Ford, my mind's running a million miles a minute."

"Let it run *ten* million miles a minute, Katie. Because it's in your hands right now to give our baby everything in the world. Summer houses. The best schools. Horses. Camps." Everything Ford had been given—everything except the kind of love he imagined most kids got for free. His own baby would have it all.

She glanced away. She was thinking about how the money might affect the baby's life, and how she would be able to tell her religious papa she wasn't having it alone, but that a surgeon from a prestigious family wanted to marry her.

"You'd move into my place until the baby's born," he added reasonably, barely able to believe what he was suggesting. "After that, it's up to you. After that, all the money belongs to the baby. But I can't do it without you. The trust is set up so that I have to be married."

"You never wanted it before?"

"I don't care about money, Katie. It's for the baby."

"And later?" Her voice was suddenly so small, so resigned that Ford wanted to retract the words...to take back that damnable Carrington power that no one could ever stand up to.

"Later, we'd work out visitation arrangements."

Her chin thrust upward a proud notch. "It would be for the baby. And, uh, I'd insist on my own bedroom."

Not a point he'd wanted to negotiate. "You said

you didn't want to see me again, Katie," he forced himself to say, stubborn pride stopping him from asking why she'd deny such insistent attraction. "Three months ago, we both agreed nothing more was going to happen between us."

Swirling the coat from her shoulders, she held it out to him, and as he took it, she edged around him, managing to open her car door. She got in and slammed the door. As she started the engine, she rolled down the window.

He squinted at her. "Katie? We're not through talking."

"I'll think things over, Ford," she promised, the line sounding oddly rehearsed. "And I'll get right back to you."

And then she simply pulled away, offering what was almost a jaunty wave. A stunned, bemused smile curled his lips as the dented white compact plunged into the night. Exiting the parking lot, she suddenly braked. Was she coming back? No. She flung open the door, leaped out as the dome light flicked on and charged to the front of the car.

"She forgot about her clothes," he whispered. Swiping them from the hood, she got inside, slammed the door and drove away. Watching the fading taillights, Ford couldn't help but murmur, "Talk about hell on wheels." But he felt strangely light, as if a cage inside him had opened and something had been set free. Was he really going to be a father in a few months? He'd expected to feel the usual fear that he'd revisit his childhood on someone else. Instead, he felt as light as air.

His and Katie's baby.

These past two years, as they'd worked together in the OR, who would have guessed it? Just as intriguing was the fact that Katie was capable of turning down ten million dollars and a marriage proposal.

Or maybe she wouldn't

"She said she'd get back to me," Ford whispered with another low, astonished chuckle. And for the first time since he'd last seen Katie, he felt genuinely curious about what would happen next.

## CHAPTER THREE

THINGS WEREN'T GOING the way Ford had imagined. Sitting cross-legged in his favorite leather armchair, he glanced around the den, shifting a cordless phone under his chin. "So, the pregnancy's been all right?" he asked, feeling oddly surprised by the missed beat of his heart when he asked.

Katie's voice softened. "Yeah. Like I said, I'm having some nausea. Nothing out of the ordinary, though. After...after we're married, I'll go to Dr. Price."

While she'd seen an obstetrician in Houston already, she needed someone here and they'd jointly decided Dr. Price would assist Ford at the birth. "Good. But are you sure you don't want to have a real wedding?"

It was probably his imagination, but as her voice came over the line, it seemed even huskier than usual, the catch of hesitation tantalizing. "You mean with flowers on the altar and me wearing a gown? You wearing a tux?"

He nodded, adding, "A flutist playing Brahms."

"You like flute music?"

"Piano's better."

Katie offered a sudden rueful laugh as if to say she shouldn't have allowed herself to get drawn into the fantasy. "I don't think we should, Ford. I mean, uh, it's *not* a real wedding."

Somehow, the reminder bothered him more than it should have, though he was amazed she'd decided to say yes. "But other people wouldn't know that. Don't you want to invite some friends, at least? You said your family's close. Shouldn't we wait until your father—"

"Comes back to town?" she interjected. "Absolutely not. That won't be for a couple more weeks. His contracting company's still on a job, and when he comes back, I want to be able to tell him the ceremony's over."

"I get the feeling he'll be sorry he missed it, Katie."

"True. But…"

When she didn't say anything, Ford prompted, "But what?"

"But he'll guess…we're not in love, Ford. He knows me like the back of his hand. Really, it's better if we just tell him we eloped when he comes back." There was a pause. "Well, sort of eloped," she added. "We do have to be married in a church. A Baptist church," she clarified.

"I'm already making arrangements, but are you positive you don't want anyone to come?"

"Not unless you want your parents…."

Ford could do without them, too. Besides, Katie was right. The marriage wasn't going to last. Why make a big deal out of it? Biting back a sigh, he chewed on his inner cheek, not about to examine his annoyance. He'd asked Katie to marry him so they could insure the trust for the baby, right? So, what was his problem? "Look, why don't we meet," he found himself saying. "You know. Get together. Maybe have some dinner. Talk about all this." Waiting a long moment, he shifted the phone from one ear to the other, then prompted, "Katie? Are you still there?"

"Still here," she said in that sweet Texas slur that set his already wild imagination rolling like a movie camera. "I think we both agree," she continued, "we really do need to keep this strictly business."

"I'm trying," he muttered. But he was also wondering what Katie was wearing. Nightgown? Sweatpants? Jeans? And what did her apartment look like? Big? Little? Throw pillows and knickknacks? Even though it was only for six months, would she miss her place while she was staying here? "Do you really think eating with me would interfere with things?"

She inhaled sharply. "Don't you think so?"

"You'll be eating with me sometimes once you move into the house," he said diplomatically.

"I know. But…" Another faintly exasperated sigh sounded before she changed the subject. "Uh, you finished working everything out with the lawyer, right?"

"Right," he said uncomfortably, wishing the situation wasn't starting to rankle. Katie hadn't wanted to get together over the past week except to work out necessary details about their marriage. Finally, he added, "Yeah. The lawyers talked. Mine said yours was good."

Actually, *brutal* was the word he'd used. Katie had lost no time in having someone carefully lay out the terms of a prenuptial agreement that would cover the baby if she and Ford divorced, which of course they would. Surprised he felt so unreasonably emotional, Ford added, "As soon as we're married, your lawyer said the paperwork would go to my parents and to Gil Gilcrest. He's the Carrington Foundation's lawyer—"

"Blane's father?"

"You know Blane Gilcrest?"

A full moment seemed to pass. "Only by name. We don't exactly run in the same crowd."

"No," he murmured, realizing Katie had probably seen Blane's name on the society page. Getting back to the issue at hand, he continued, "Sure you don't want to get together to take the edge off this? We're doing the right thing, Katie, but..."

He thought he heard her voice catch again. "But?"

He glanced toward the red-carpeted steps leading upstairs, hardly wanting to contemplate the amount of time he'd spent deciding which sheets should go on the bed Katie would soon be using. He'd settled on red satin. "But it's strange to be sitting here, planning a divorce before we're even married," he admitted. Strange, too, to think Katie Topper would soon be sharing his house, sleeping right down the hall from him.

She exhaled another quick breath. "Strange or not, it's what we're doing, isn't it?"

Yes. But she didn't have to sound so...well, businesslike. He understood, he even knew she was right, but that didn't stop him from wanting her where she'd been months ago, naked and shivering in his bed, smiling at him in the moonlight flooding the room.

To his ears, the words sounded lame. "I'd just like to see you before the wedding."

There was a long pause, and then she said, "Why?"

Why? After the night they'd shared, how could she ask? "So we'd feel more comfortable with each other when you move in."

"I'll think about it and get back to you," she said.

"You do that." Even though hers was probably the wisest course, her businesslike tone, the cold legality of dealing with lawyers, the fact that she didn't want to see him—it was all so frustrating.

Right before the phone went dead, she conceded, "Oh, I don't know, Ford. Maybe we could get together just once. Like I said, I'll get back to you."

"She'll get back to me," Ford muttered to the dial tone. He was hardly used to this treatment from women and he found he didn't particularly like it.

STANDING NEXT TO FORD at the altar in a small Baptist church that wasn't but six miles away from the one her papa attended so faithfully every Sunday, Katie tried to tell herself that to refuse ten million dollars and a well-known Austin surname for the baby would have been to look a gift horse in the mouth—a cardinal sin in Texas, if there was one.

Not to mention she'd now be allowed to live.

She shuddered to think of her papa's reaction if she'd had to announce she was unmarried and pregnant. So what if she'd been secretly enamored of Ford Carrington ever since she'd met him? So what if the rose Ford brought her today tempted her to imagine she was wearing a gown and he was wearing a tux.

Or that a flutist and pianist were playing Brahams and her friends and family were here. Yes…Ford loved her. Tonight, they'd be sharing a bed.

*Stop it, Katie!*

Smoothing her best sage dress, she curled her fingers tightly around the rose stem, feeling a pang that was sad and wistful by turns. Moments from now, it would look as if her every secret fantasy about Ford Carrington had come true. But fantasy was exactly what this marriage was, and she simply couldn't afford to forget that.

When Ford's admiring gaze drifted over the knit dress, taking in the nipped waist and V neck, she vowed she'd never fall for the charms he'd begun displaying while they planned the wedding. Although his proposal was motivated by a desire to secure their baby's future, Ford obviously wanted more closeness. It was only natural, she told herself. She was carrying their child, after all, but she had no doubt that Ford's new feelings would pass. While she wouldn't forget how easily he'd said he didn't love her—as if he never could. Even his own grandfather had known Ford wasn't the marrying kind, which was why he'd offered this enticing trust fund for Ford's firstborn as incentive.

It had worked, too, Katie thought, nervously glancing around the church. Her eyes settled on Ford, who looked as handsome as the devil and smelled like heaven. She wished she was half as composed, but seeing him out of hospital pants and a lab coat always increased her anxiety to a point that was unbearable.

Wistfulness washed over her as she took in the fit of a black suit that brought out his jet hair and eyes.

Beneath the jacket, against a white pressed shirt, a silver and black striped tie rippled, fastened with a pearl pin. Her knees weakened. She was the first person in her family to go to college, and yet she hadn't been smart enough to know sleeping with Ford wouldn't get him out of her system. Now the voice of reason said marrying him would probably make things worse.

What other choice did she have, though? Surely, over these next months, she could keep her emotional distance, couldn't she? For the sake of their child? She darted her eyes around furtively. Having no one at the church helped. The fewer people brought into this charade, the better. Catching her gaze, Ford smiled.

She tried to smile back, but her rapid heart rate was causing too much distress. Tasteful and expensive, everything about Ford down to his Italian loafers was a reminder that the man let astounding sums roll off his tongue as simply as breathing…sums such as ten million dollars. Katie had seen the number written on legal contracts, but it remained nothing more than a nonsensical looking one followed by an endless string of zeros. All the world's money meant nothing next to the love Katie was going to give this child, but she did hope the Carrington name would open doors, should their child ever want to go through them.

*Lord, Katie,* she suddenly thought. *Listen to yourself! Come to your senses and end this right here. Just tell the minister and Ford that it's over, that you've changed your mind….*

Her throat felt suddenly raw. For two years, she'd secretly wondered about Ford Carrington. How did he spend his time? What did he like to eat? She was loath to admit it, but she used to shut her eyes late at night when she was in bed and imagine Ford was touching her. And then, one magical night, he did....

She ended the thought right there. No, no matter what, she couldn't afford to get confused about the true nature of their relationship. There couldn't be one slip. Not one seductive glance. Not one kiss. No brushing against each other in the hallways of the house they were about to share. Definitely not sex.

Never.

And she'd survive it, because she knew she was doing the right thing for the baby. With a start, she realized the minister, a heavy, ruddy-cheeked man, had ceased reading from a prayer book. She thought he'd said, "Do you, Katharine Topper...?"

Her heart thudded dully. Too many feelings were vying for dominance: excitement, curiosity and panic. Her voice seemed to come from far away. "Yes...yes, I do."

Moments later, when she heard Dr. Ford Carrington calmly state, "I do," everything seemed to spin. Attempting to steady herself, she glanced around the church, taking in its rough-hewn pews, Mexican tile floor and the plain windows through which weak winter sunlight streamed.

Maybe she'd feel this way until she was divorced.

When she'd called Ford with her decision, she'd kept things to the point, all business, but once she'd set the ball rolling, things progressed with a logic all their own, as if they'd been planned. Katie felt it almost created the illusion that she was in control. Everything seemed delicately orchestrated, like a perfectly choreographed operation, but this time a prayer book was their X ray and wedding rings their instruments.

But now she realized it wasn't over.

This was only the beginning. Seeing the ring on Katie's finger would appease her papa, as would his hearing about this church wedding, but Katie suspected she was nowhere close to what the Carringtons might desire in a daughter-in-law. Ford was their only son, the sole Carrington heir, and if they had any inkling that a wedding ceremony was in process, maybe they'd use their considerable power to stop it. Was that the real reason Ford hadn't invited them?

While he evaded questions about his family, she'd been surprised to find him so interested in hers. Her papa was still in Dallas, but her younger brothers, Jem and Gary, were at home, living on the farm, and Ford had asked to meet them. She'd finally agreed, since it would make news of a later elopement less startling, but she hadn't expected Ford's easy adjustment to Topper routines. Single-handedly, he'd shod horses, mucked out stalls, then helped her brothers train a two-year-old mare to load in the horse trailer.

By the time they'd gone trail riding, Katie was so unsettled that she meanly put Ford on a contrary gelding named Huge Luther, only to have Ford's masterful handling of the spiteful animal leave her stewing in her own juices. Later, while she cooked dinner, the men announced they were going skinny-dipping in the lake. Since the temperature was hovering at sixty, Katie found herself muttering that she hoped they froze off their privates. It would serve them right.

Ford had laughed.

And despite her determination not to warm to him again, Katie had found herself laughing, too. Hours later, his hair still damp, she'd watched him mop gravy from a plate with a biscuit just as her brothers did. "Best meal I've ever eaten, Carrot Top," he'd said, grinning.

"She's a great cook," Jem had agreed, slowly pulling at his red handlebar mustache.

"Just wish she'd come home more often," Gary added. "I'm starving. Papa can't boil water. I think I lost twenty pounds when she was staying in Houston."

Katie had glanced over plates piled high with fried steaks and gravy, red beans and grits, and her lips had curled into a teasing smile. "Thought it might be too plebeian for Ford's taste," she'd teased. "Aren't you used to snails and fish eggs or some such?"

"Guess you'll find out soon enough."

Standing at the altar, Katie decided soon enough was maybe *too* soon. Tomorrow night, after her first day back at Maitland Maternity, she and Ford were supposed to tell his folks the news, and Katie figured a mess was going to hit the fan. Ford had made an appointment for the two of them to meet with Yvonne and David Carrington before a Carrington Foundation party, where the annual allocations of funds to various charities would be announced.

*An appointment.*

That's what Ford had called it, and the time was precisely seven forty-five. Apparently, Ford was being allotted a grand total of fifteen minutes to announce a marriage and coming baby. Not that his folks knew that. Still, what sort of parents needed to pen notations in black books before meeting an only son? When Toppers wanted an audience, they grabbed telephones, shrieked up flights of stairs or— if all else failed—clanged the old iron bell that hung from a tree in the front yard.

Suddenly, Katie drew another sharp breath. Ford was lifting her hand. "With this ring, I thee wed...."

What they were doing was insane, she thought as the ring, so cool and smooth, slid onto her finger. How could she be so close to Ford—and yet so far away? Married—but not really married? Sleeping in his house—yet not in the bed they had already shared three months ago? It would be so easy to grow to love that spacious house, those beautiful horses....

*Which is why you should have said no, Katie Topper!* Or was she Katie Carrington? She swallowed hard, barely getting saliva past the lump in her throat. The simple gold band she'd chosen rested against a diamond engagement ring Ford insisted she wear, and when she glanced at the nesting rings, the air in her lungs evaporated, leaving her strangely light-headed.

"I now join you, husband and wife...."

It was over. At least she thought it was. Katie was barely aware of thanking and shaking hands with the minister, who vanished into a hallway. Lifting an agitated hand to her hair—she realized it was her left hand, since she could feel the weight of the rings— she nervously finger-combed the waves, then shot Ford a quick, uneasy smile. Just as he smiled back, she almost ceased to breathe. She needed air. Abruptly, she turned to go and was three-quarters down the center aisle, almost to fresh oxygen, when

Ford's warm strong hand settled on her shoulder. "Think you forgot something, Katie."

She turned around. If the thumb gently rubbing her exposed collarbone hadn't stolen her remaining breath, the calm, solemn expression of Ford's eyes would have. She frowned. "What?" she murmured. "What did we forget?"

"This, Katie."

Ford's hands glided around her waist, and she felt a flinch of nerve and sinew, the flex of long fingers when he pulled her toward him. It was only natural to tilt her head. Only natural for Ford to angle his downward. Their eyes met, and his were like the brown of newly turned earth. Lightly, he licked his lips. Hers parted, just a fraction.

A second passed in which she could have moved, and when she didn't, he leaned down and kissed her, thoroughly and deeply, proving that whatever lessons he'd learned three months ago, he hadn't forgotten them. Every pretty little speech she'd rehearsed in case this happened vanished with the onslaught of Ford's tongue. Leaning her head back, feeling that cool sensual invasion, she tasted mint and drew in his scent until she was helpless to do anything but wreathe her arms around his neck.

With the deepening kiss, a transparent line seemed to stretch between her and Ford, as if a kiss could keep them connected even if they were miles apart. She was fishing, simultaneously casting and drowning, and as the last vestiges of sense swirled like water from her body, she felt forever lost. Her tongue stroked his. Her hands crept upward. Her fingers splayed, slipping into dark, thick, silken hair. His hands dropped, eliciting a soft, near-silent whimper as they curved ever so slowly over her hips, bringing a rush of wicked temptation that hardly belonged in church.

With thoughts of their whereabouts, Katie's lost senses came rushing back. Just moments ago she'd sworn to herself she'd never do this! she thought as the long, transparent line between them zipped backward, as if spinning around a reel. Somehow, she forced herself to jerk breathlessly away. Inches from hers, Ford's eyes looked dreamy, heavily lidded and nearly black. His lips were wet. His voice was husky. "That was some kiss, Mrs. Carrington."

*Mrs. Carrington.* When her knees weakened at the words, she decided she could kill Ford for saying that right now. *Mrs. Carrington.* Why did it have to sound so damnably good? The kiss had been far better than decent, too.

"Some kiss," he repeated.

Sure was. "Unfortunately," she whispered miserably.

There was a long strained silence.

With her heart still beating out of control, she primly added in a hushed tone, "I just thank God we were in church." What if they'd been alone in the home they were about to share? Katie didn't mean for her vocal cords to quiver, but they did, destroying her credibility. "What do you think you're doing, Ford?"

"Kissing you, Katie." If her voice was wind whistling through high grass, his was dry husks rustling in a quiet breeze. "Just like you were kissing me back."

*Oh, please, don't make this difficult.* It took everything she had to muster the voice of reason. "We have an agreement. Signed, sealed, delivered. Remember?"

His steady eyes smoldered with intent, and his lips quirked in slow bemusement that said he knew how much she secretly wanted him. Her eyes drifted up the planes of his cheeks to the sharp edges of his cheekbones, and she wished he didn't look quite so gorgeous, and that his voice wasn't quite so scratchily male when he murmured, "An agreement? I thought I *was* being agreeable, Katie."

Two seconds ago, with his mouth locked on hers, she would have agreed to anything. Now her throat felt raw. Somehow, having this man's baby growing inside her had made her feel almost as if he belonged to her. It wasn't true, though. Ford was his own man. Straightening her knees, she braced them slightly apart, steadying herself. "We've talked about all this, Ford."

"Our lawyers did, at any rate."

She nodded. She was keeping her apartment, only moving some clothes into his house for the next six months, just until the baby was born. "We have a contract. A prenup. Not to mention a verbal understanding."

The irritating, bemused tilt of his lips lifted another fraction, and his voice turned to pure silk. "Sure you read all the fine print, Katie?"

Her lips parted in astonishment. Had Ford slipped in a stipulation about her fulfilling the usual obligations of a wife? she wondered, her heart fluttering. Had he tricked her somehow? Would she be absolutely forced to make love with him? By law? Would there be no way out? No way to refuse?

After a moment, she admitted to herself that having legally sanctioned sex with Ford had real appeal.

Then she shook her head to clear it of confusion. "No...I hired an excellent attorney." He'd reviewed every scrap of paper having to do with the baby's trust fund and this marriage. The only thing they hadn't yet done was approach Gil Gilcrest, since the baby's funds would come from the Carrington Foundation. As soon as they told Ford's folks, they'd finish the paperwork. "Our lawyers went over our prenup with a fine-tooth comb," she assured him. "For my part, I was told it said nothing about..." She fought to control it, but a blush colored her face, anyway. "Extras."

Looking thoughtful, Ford lifted a hand and stroked his knuckles across her cheek with unnerving confidence. "A shame," he whispered.

She didn't know which was more unnerving—that silken touch or the fact that she felt boxed into the position of playing the prude. Ford knew better, of course. Three months ago, she'd done things no prude would. Worse, she still wanted to do those things. Her usually trustworthy voice came out sounding unforgivably faint. "Shame?"

"You like kissing me, don't you, Katie."

It wasn't really a question. Her heart hammered. "Maybe." There was no use denying it. "But we can't forget why we're doing this...what this marriage means. This is about our baby's needs."

"But what about my needs?" Before she could respond, Ford added, "And what about yours? I want those extras, Katie. All the bells and whistles. Since we're married now, I don't see why we can't enjoy ourselves for the next six months.''

He sure didn't waste time. She stared at him a long moment. Forcing herself to breathe slowly, she tried to calm her rapidly beating heart. He made sharing a bed sound so practical that she had a wild impulse to throttle him. ''Your first proposal stunned me,'' she said, forcing a cool tone. ''But this?''

He didn't look the least concerned. ''Why not enjoy what we've already discovered we both like to share?''

''Are you really saying you want six months of casual sex?''

''Don't you?''

That wasn't the point. ''I'm beginning to think you can really make love the way you operate, Ford.''

His penetrating eyes pinned hers. ''You don't have to *think* about how I make love, Katie,'' he said. ''You already know.''

She sure did, and the memories were making her bones feel like rubber. ''Are you going to ignore our agreement?''

''No. But how are you beginning to think I make love?''

Her temper flared. ''Without emotion.'' Deep down, maybe she'd simply wanted more from him, a promise of a deepening relationship, a friendship. If he'd offered that, maybe she'd have said yes, like a fool. Defensive heat rose in her cheeks. ''Let's leave it right here, Ford. We're walking out of this church together. We're going to spend the next six months together. But nothing's going to happen.''

The eyes that flickered over her sent another knot of heat to her belly. It coiled at the core of her, then came unsprung and leaped, prancing through her veins. "Believe me," he said, "if something happens, it'll be at your insistence, Katie."

That was exactly what she was afraid of.

"WHAT HAVE I DONE?" Ford muttered, kicking off the covers and glancing around his dark bedroom. Medical school had taught him to sleep anytime, anywhere. He'd done it on hard floors, lumpy cots, even standing up. Once, during a particularly grueling rotation, he'd been discovered dozing in an oversize basket of linens in a hospital laundry room.

But that was before Katie Topper Carrington. Now it was three a.m., and as tempting as it was to pace before her doorway until she ventured out in the skimpy nightgown he kept imagining, Ford wasn't giving an inch. For the sake of pride—and Carringtons had plenty—he could keep up the same disinterested front Katie had displayed earlier at the church.

"For now," he whispered, still tasting their kiss. Sure, she was right. They had an agreement. But sooner or later, she'd recall what had happened between them three months ago. It was so powerful it had sparked new life...which meant it was plenty powerful enough to lead her to his bed again. Next time, he'd cradle her even closer, lie with her like spoons and run his palms over her belly, knowing he'd be the first man to touch their child....

He'd had no idea that being near a woman who was pregnant with his baby would have this effect on him.

He had no idea what to do at this hour, either. He got up, pulled on worn jeans, an old comfortable cotton sweater and jacket, then headed for the stables. He saddled a thoroughbred gelding named Go-Boy, led him into the ring, and as he shoved a boot into a stirrup, he tried not to notice moonlight catching the flash of a wedding ring when his fist closed around the pommel.

Suddenly, he swallowed hard. He was married. His wife was pregnant. They were having a baby in six months. He could barely believe it. His heart catching as he blew out a sigh of pure sexual frustration, he abruptly swung into the saddle, deciding the only saving grace was that the house was huge. Not large enough that he and Katie could stay lost for six months, though. Eventually they'd probably be at each other's throats. But what choice did they have? The Carrington trust was worded so that Ford had to be married to his firstborn's mother, and eyebrows would be raised if he and Katie were married but not living together. At least he'd put her in the bedroom farthest away from him, down a long hallway, so he couldn't hear her footsteps or the running shower.

He heard them anyway.

In fact, he imagined he heard much more: the whisper of the knit sage dress falling to the floor as she undressed for bed, a soft sigh of effort as she picked up the dress, wrapped it around a hanger, then hung it in the closet. An enticing rustle of fabric as she pulled a nightgown over her head. Did silk, cotton or lace shimmy over her hips? Or was she sleeping naked?

Ford stared toward the house he'd named Skycrest.

Through the trees, its white paint gleamed under the exterior security lamps and moonlight. The night was cold, the moon not quite full, not the way it had been three months ago, the first night Katie slept here…the night she'd become pregnant.

Who would have guessed a second night could be so punishing? Moments after they arrived, she'd retired as if he'd bitten her, saying the day's excitement had worn her out. "The *day*," he muttered.

It was the night that was doing him in.

But then, he was a man. If the decision was left solely to him, he and Katie would have hit the sheets before sundown. No one was more adept at severing emotions than a Carrington, however; maybe that was why they'd all become doctors. And if Katie demanded a marriage in name only, that's what he'd give her. Ford just hoped she was suffering for it.

Urging the gelding into a trot, Ford thought about how his parents had drummed the need for prenuptial agreements into his head. Wouldn't they be shocked to learn it was Ford's wife who'd demanded one? A wife who had nothing to lose financially—and everything to gain?

A wife. *His* wife. A woman who was going to love and care for their baby, and whom he was now tied to, no matter where else life might take them.

Ignoring a ripple of emotion, Ford kicked his heels harder until cold air whistled past the gelding's shuddering flanks and hoofbeats grew from a whisper on soft earth to a pounding vibration. Breath fluttered through the horse's quivering nostrils as he broke into a gallop. Tightening his thighs, Ford felt wind ruffling through his hair and shirt, and even though he wasn't proud of the crude turn of his thoughts, he wished he was riding Katie, not a horse.

He stared toward the house again. Silhouetted black against the moonlit night, trees framed her darkened, uninviting window. He knew he was wishing for a light to snap on; just as surely, he knew it wouldn't. Katie didn't care about him. She was probably sound asleep. No, there was no use denying he'd done the one thing he'd vowed he never would: married a woman who didn't love him.

Even worse, every new fact he discovered about his wife made him want her even more. The Topper farm was a small bedraggled forty-acre spread with a tumbledown barn and countless stray cats and dogs Katie had taken in, but at a glance, Ford had realized it was far more homey than the huge, empty house his parents had named Lincoln's Landing. He'd pushed to visit the place, and even now felt another rush of annoyance that she hadn't initially wanted him to go.

Like so many people at Maitland Maternity, Katie's college-age brothers hung the moon by her, and it wasn't just because she helped them financially, though she did. Love was palpable in the Toppers' modest, four-bedroom farmhouse. Ford had felt it in the air. Still, you couldn't make people love you if they weren't so inclined. Ford had learned that long ago. Even if he spent the next six months charming Katie, he'd most likely wind up stuck with exactly what he'd settled for: a loveless marriage for name and money. The exact kind of marriage Katie also disdained.

Silently, Ford cursed his legacy. The Carrington

name was an albatross around his neck. Without it, he and Katie wouldn't have lowered their principles. Whatever they got after this situation probably served them both right. Leaning lower over the mane to better feel the rude wind, he reminded himself of something he also believed, that the coming baby deserved the legacy, for whatever it was worth. Maybe he or she would figure out what Ford never had—how to use it to find happiness.

But could Ford handle six months of living with Katie? Of imagining her in the shower? Wanting her in bed? And how would things be later? he wondered, his heart twisting. He'd delivered so many babies, saved the lives of so many more. But only this one was his. Could he help shape this life better than his father had shaped his?

Suddenly, he thought he saw a shadow in Katie's window. It brought a flicker of far-off memory, of how, when he was a kid, he'd stop playing and stare up at his father's study window, thinking his father was watching him. He wasn't, any more than Katie was. The glimpse he'd thought was of a white nightgown was really only his imagination, and yet it stoked the fire in Ford's belly. In that instant he was hungry to claim what he'd missed for three torturous months, what he felt was his due as Katie's husband…a hunger he'd never felt before the night he'd spent with her. Something that he imagined felt like love.

BEING SLEEP DEPRIVED didn't stop Katie from appreciating the cards, balloons and gossip awaiting her the next day at Maitland Maternity. She hadn't realized how much she missed the snapshots she'd left on her desk, especially the black-and-white eight-by-ten of her mama, or the bad decaf coffee perking in the kitchen. Dr. Nelson had left a note, welcoming her to his team, and after a grueling morning in surgery, Katie was finally breaking for lunch. She was just about to make good on a promise to chat with Beth Maitland, who ran the clinic's day care, when she was waylaid at the nursery.

"Really, Katie," said Megan Maitland, the family matriarch who'd started the hospital. "We're so glad you're back from Houston."

Glancing away from the newborns on the other side of the window, Katie smiled. "Thank you so much." Just as she was about to continue on to Beth's office, Connor O'Hara, Megan's nephew, joined her and Megan, and although he addressed his aunt, Katie couldn't find a polite way to excuse herself.

Managing to stifle a yawn, she looked through the window again. All shapes, sizes and colors, the babies made her grin sleepily. Truly, she thought, no one made shut-eye look quite so good as a newborn. She couldn't wait to hold her own child. Unbidden, an image of Ford came to mind, and she was glad he'd be handling the delivery. Her grin turned into a lopsided smile. What would it be like to deliver your own child? She guessed she'd soon see the joy of it in Ford's eyes. As bothersome as the man's kisses were, she was definitely glad he was going to have that unforgettable experience.

Releasing a soft sigh she thought of Ford's sumptuous guest room, with its thick green carpet that melted her toes and the canopied bed piled high with blue and gold tapestried pillows. It was as soft as a cloud, which meant her wayward mind was the problem. How could she lie on red satin sheets without remembering the firm grasp of Ford's lips, or the heat and muscle of his body?

Ford must have been equally restless. In the middle of the night, she'd heard hammering hooves. She'd gotten up and stared out the window and down the sloping lawn to the riding ring, watching him gallop under the moonlight. Seeing his body hunched and taut, she'd shuddered, remembering how those legs had felt, bare and flexing against hers.

Ford had looked up. She'd felt like an idiot, or like some lovesick woman in a Gothic novel, her stomach all aflutter. She'd gasped, but instead of stepping back, she'd pressed her fingertips to the glass. And then she'd slipped back into bed. Alone. She was just as lonely as Ford. But she meant what she'd said. She'd live with him and share household responsibilities for six months, but she wasn't going to confuse the issue by sleeping with him again. Being that close to him—loving him, carrying his child—would too easily break her heart. *Unless he changed his mind,* a little voice said, *unless he said he loved you.*

Startled, she looked up. "Hmm?"

Megan Maitland was smoothing her white hair, her snapping dark blue eyes on Katie. "I said you look a little tired, Katie. Nervous about your first day back?"

*More nervous about secretly marrying your chief pediatric surgeon, and about becoming a mother.* She'd removed the rings before coming to work, of course, since she and Ford had agreed to tell their families first, but now, fighting a flush, Katie wondered how hospital staff would react to the news. "How could I be nervous?" she managed to reply lightly. "I love this place. It's my home away from home. I don't think I realized how much until today."

"We've missed you, too, Katie," Megan returned. "When Dr. Nelson said you'd been offered a job in Houston, I was terrified you'd take it. If you ever feel tempted, please see me first. I can personally assure you that Maitland Maternity intends to match any offers."

"Thanks again," said Katie.

She was about to make her exit when Megan smiled, this time placing a loving hand on Connor's shoulder. For the first time, Katie took a good look at the man. He had blue eyes, and his hair was dark, like Ford's. He was about forty, handsome in a weathered outdoorsy way—and definitely grist for Maitland Maternity's gossip mill. There were other stories, of course. Around the time Katie left town, folks had been trying to discover the identity of the abandoned baby boy who was being called Cody. He'd been found at the hospital just as Megan was preparing to announce the hospital's upcoming twenty-fifth anniversary bash. Since then, a number of women had come forward to claim the baby, but none had proven themselves the mother.

Insofar as the scoop on Connor went, Katie still hadn't gotten the entire story straight. It was a doozy. She'd been told that Connor O'Hara was Megan Maitland's nephew, the son of Jack O'Hara and Clarise Maitland O'Hara, a couple that had moved from Austin to Amarillo many years ago, severing all ties

with the Maitland family. Now Connor's sudden, re-
cent appearance in Austin was making people curious.

*As if you don't have enough secrets of your own!*
Katie chided herself. Not that her situation was anywhere near as mysterious as Connor's. Apparently,
Megan had set him up in one of the family's condos
and opened a hefty bank account for him, since he'd
had financial difficulties after the death of his mother,
Clarise. He'd been forced to sell his ranch, and rumor
had it that a woman he'd loved had left him.

Looking away from the babies, Connor caught Katie's eye. He smiled. "Wish I had one of my own."

Sighing, Megan pressed her fingertips to the glass.
"Aren't they simply wonderful?"

"I could watch them all day," Katie agreed, her
gaze traveling over the tiny, crinkled faces, cute knit
caps and socks. Gliding a palm over her belly, she
felt a sadness twist inside her, then fuse with joy.
Why couldn't her baby be going home with parents
who were crazy about each other? Folks who couldn't
keep their eyes or hands to themselves? Who, along
with good old-fashioned lust, had fully committed to
each other? That's what a baby deserved.

For long moments, Connor and Megan spoke in
low tones, and only when she heard Connor gasp did
Katie turn her head from the babies again. "Janelle?"
Connor whispered, obviously stunned.

Katie watched as a pretty young woman with long
brown hair and dark eyes approached them at break-
neck speed down the empty hallway. The closer she
got, the more Katie could tell that she was over-
wrought; her nursing instincts went on alert, but the
woman didn't seem ill. Stopping breathlessly in front

of Connor, she gaped at him, looking equally shocked. "Connor? What are you doing here?"

*This must be the woman who left Connor heart-broken before he came to Austin,* Katie thought. It was a gut-level reaction. Quite possibly wrong. But if so, what was the woman doing here? It was none of Katie's business, but she was riveted.

"Janelle…I can't believe this," Connor was saying. "How did you know I was here?"

"I didn't!" A quick toss of Janelle's head sent brown hair flying. "Connor, you told me that you and your aunt Megan were estranged. That's her, isn't it? Your aunt Megan?"

"Yes," he replied, his eyes fixing on Janelle's.

Hers darkened as if she half expected Connor to lie to her, and Katie thought a silent signal passed between Megan and Connor…as if something was afoot that the older woman didn't want Katie to know.

"Janelle, I'm sorry," Megan said swiftly. "You've taken us by surprise. Please, let me welcome you to Maitland Maternity. Connor's told me so much about you." She turned to Katie. "This is Janelle, Katie. A woman…a friend of Connor's." Smiling, she added, "Janelle, I'd like you to meet one of our nurses, Katie Topper."

*Carrington,* Katie silently added.

Janelle offered a quick, distracted nod.

"Perhaps we should all go to my office?" Megan suggested.

Knowing the "we" didn't include her, Katie turned, but before she could move away, Janelle grabbed her arm, her eyes darting to Katie's for support. "I'm not going anywhere," the woman announced. "I want to have my say first. There's always two sides to a story."

"I'm sure there are," murmured Katie politely, wishing Janelle wasn't holding her in a death grip, especially since Megan Maitland obviously wanted to take this exchange elsewhere. "Uh…Janelle, I'm sure everyone will hear you out, if you'll just go with Connor to Ms. Maitland's office."

"I said I'm not going anywhere—" Janelle's tone was almost accusatory. "I broke up with Connor because we were having problems communicating."

Feeling the grasp tighten, Katie darted her eyes around the hallway. Thankfully, it was still empty, so no one else was witnessing what should have been a private discussion. Katie flashed an apologetic glance at Megan while Janelle rambled on. "See, Connor was working all the time…."

Katie was so busy trying to disengage the woman's fingers without causing a scene that she barely heard the rest. Why hadn't the woman taken Megan's cue to get out of the hallway? It was almost as if she wanted Katie to stay and hear her. Or more likely, she feared Connor and Megan would gang up on her for some reason. Katie suddenly gasped, hearing the word "pregnant." Her mind caught up a second later, when Janelle said, "I found out and then I tried to contact him. I hoped the baby would interest him as much as his ranch."

Connor seemed stunned, barely aware they were still in the hallway. "You were pregnant, Janelle? When?"

"Pregnant?" Megan echoed. Then once more she reiterated, "Can we please go to my office?"

The woman didn't seem to hear. Her eyes skated nervously to the newborns. "I tried to contact you when I found out," she rushed on, her eyes riveted on Connor. "But you sold the ranch, didn't you? There was no forwarding address...nothing. So, I brought the baby here."

Connor's eyes were flickering hungrily over the woman. He looked as if he was still in love with her, Katie thought. "Oh, Lord," he said, his voice strained. "You had a baby? Our baby?"

Janelle looked half fearful, a fish out of water, a woman out of her element among the powerful Maitlands. "I named him Chase. I had no choice but to leave him here at the time. I knew he'd be taken care of, but now—"

Her voice broke, and the tears shining in her eyes tore at Katie's heart. She'd pulled together enough threads of the conversation to understand that Janelle had been pregnant and unmarried. Katie could relate to that experience. But Janelle looked much more vulnerable.

"May we *please* go into my office," Megan said once more.

Janelle, her hand still wrapped around Katie's arm, barely seemed to hear. "On the news, I keep hearing about women coming forward, trying to claim the baby I left here." Her eyes shifted worriedly between Connor, Megan and Katie. "I couldn't let some stranger take my baby." A teetering tear rolled down her cheek.

"Nobody's taking your baby," Megan assured her, looking stunned herself. "Little Cody...that's him. Oh, my God. I didn't even make the connection until now. That's your son, isn't it? The baby we found on the steps?''

Janelle nodded. "His name's Chase. Chase O'Hara.'' Her voice was spiked with sudden panic. "And don't worry. I can prove it.''

"That's what the C.O. on his bracelet stands for,'' Megan murmured. "Chase O'Hara.'' *Connor's son!* Megan added silently. It had been enough of a shock when Connor had shown up a few months ago—Megan's firstborn child. All these years she'd thought he was dead; that's what her father had told her—what he had wanted her to believe. And now this—little Cody—little Chase was her grandson. Her mind spun wildly. Only Connor knew the truth—Connor and her daughter Ellie. Megan prayed Connor wouldn't be foolish enough to confide in Janelle—at least not in Katie's presence. She needed time to think, Megan realized. Time to decide what to do next. At the moment what she needed most was privacy.

"Really,'' Megan repeated, this time more adamantly. "My office.''

An embarrassed flush stole over Janelle's face, as if she only now realized she had an audience. Katie felt the iron grip around her arm loosen, and she murmured, "Why don't I leave you all alone?''

Megan looked relieved. "Thank you so much, Katie.''

"No problem.'' As she headed down the hallway, Katie realized how much she'd missed the intrigue and gossip that were always a part of the hospital. Come what may between her and Maitland Maternity's chief pediatric surgeon, it was sure good to be back home.

# CHAPTER FOUR

LIFTING A HAND from the steering wheel, Ford thrust
it through his already tousled hair, then tapped his
fingertips on the dashboard to a Hank Williams cas-
sette Katie had shoved into the tape deck. "So after
you started to leave, this woman—Janelle—she
pulled you back?"

Peering through the windshield, where orange and
purple clouds drifted behind a burst of red sun, Katie
tried to catch a glimpse of Ford's parents' home.
"Yeah. I was walking down the hall when she
grabbed me by the arm again." Katie blew out a sigh,
unable to stop her eyes from sweeping over Ford in
a quick caress. "Tightly," she added. "I swear, I
think the marks are still there. Anyway, right there in
the hallway, Janelle lifted up Connor's shirt. Sure
enough, there was a birthmark on the man's stomach,
just like she'd claimed."

Ford's eyes shifted from the windshield. "A birthmark?"

Katie nodded. "Crescent-shaped. Just like the one
on the baby. Megan took that as proof that Connor's
really the baby's father."

"Megan didn't say anything about the birthmark to
the press when they first found the baby," Ford said
thoughtfully. "She figured whoever claimed the baby

could identify him that way. I remember looking at it when I examined him the day he was found."

"You and I weren't the only ones who saw it, Ford. The baby's nurse, the day-care workers.... The fact that it was kept a secret is a real testimony to the kind of loyalty Megan inspires in people."

He nodded. "The only trouble is it's no proof of paternity, since birthmarks aren't inherited."

Katie shook her head worriedly, "I tried to tell Megan. I mean, in school I never heard of such a case, though one's probably documented somewhere."

Ford chuckled appreciatively, the warm rich sound filling the car. "In medicine, everything's documented somewhere."

"Megan said it's unusual, but not unheard of, that a birthmark's inherited." Katie shrugged. "Guess we'll find out. I said I'd be happy to give Janelle a maternity test whenever she's ready."

Ford frowned. "She didn't want one today?"

"No," said Katie. "I told her it would only take a minute, but I guess she was in too much of a hurry to see the baby."

Ford's voice warmed. "You can't blame her for that."

For a second, the sudden, wistful tugging of her heart seemed to make it swell, and Katie didn't trust herself to respond. In her wildest fantasies, she'd never imagined Ford being so excited about having their child, but he was. Foolishly, she couldn't quit wishing his excitement extended to her, but if she hadn't accidentally become pregnant, Ford would never have considered marrying her. Two years ago, when they'd first started working together, she'd hung around after surgeries, trying to talk to him, but he hadn't seemed interested so she'd given up.

"After Janelle takes the test," she began, picking up the conversation, "Megan's going to let her use a guest cottage on her property."

"What happened after Janelle showed you the birthmark?"

"Nothing. I took her and Connor to the day care to see Chase—that's the baby's real name—and left them there."

"Alone?"

"With Lizzie and Cheryl."

"Hmm. Hear anything else juicy today?"

Katie slid her eyes toward him again. It was tempting to tell him the rest, but Katie had promised to stay mum. As soon as she'd left the day care, she'd headed for Beth's office, just as promised, only to find Beth brushing back her long dark curly hair, her eyes redrimmed from crying.

"Oh, Katie," she'd cried. "Could you come in and shut the door? It's Brandon."

"Dumont?" Katie had asked, closing the door behind her.

Beth weepily confided that the wealthy Austinite had just called to break their engagement. "He's marrying Brianne," Beth explained.

Although Katie had only met Brandon briefly, her heart went out to Beth. Her friend was devastated. Fighting a sudden panic, Katie wondered how she would feel once the baby was born and her marriage to Ford came to an end.

Realizing Ford was smiling at her, Katie forced

herself to smile back. "Nice to share hospital scuttle-butt with somebody whose curiosity equals mine."

There was no denying the hint of huskiness in his voice. "We do gossip well together, don't we, Katie?"

He was implying they did other things well together, too. She nodded, and as they neared his parents' estate, she glanced away, growing quieter. All afternoon, the secret of their marriage and pregnancy had burned inside her like a fire. Announcing the news to Yvonne and David Carrington was unnerving, to say the least, and once their marriage became public knowledge, everybody at the hospital was going to have a field day.

*Anyone would be nervous.* Anyone but Ford, it seemed. Watching him, Katie noted he drove a car exactly the way he operated, with seemingly effortless concentration. "Bet you've never even had a fender bender," she challenged, the change of topic calming her.

He flashed a smile. "Jealous?"

Yesterday he'd remarked that her car had as many nicks as a teenage boy. Rifling fingers absently through her hair and praying the moist air didn't make the curls frizz, she scoffed. "You could have bought two of my cars for this one."

Ford tried to look offended, glancing around the interior of his loaded Toyota Camry. "True," he offered. "And I get the impression you think *your* car's got more character."

"If you think missing a side-view mirror indicates character, then maybe we should get rid of your front bumper."

He chuckled. "Now, that would constitute real class."

Lightly, she couldn't help but say, "Good thing class isn't one of my concerns."

He glanced across the seat. "You think it's mine?"

"Sorry," she murmured. "I'm taking my nervousness out on you."

"No, you're not sorry, Katie," he countered without rancor, another amused smile curling his lips. "Spit it out. You think I was born with a silver spoon in my mouth."

She couldn't help but laugh. "Weren't you?"

"Maybe. But it didn't buy my way out of life's troubles."

"That's the thing about silver spoons," she said, shooting him an easy grin. "They'd be more likely to stir trouble up."

His eyes lingered on her longer than they should have before returning to the road. "C'mon, Katie. I know you're nervous, but loosen up. We're not even staying. We're in, we're out. I promise."

The speedy way he intended to introduce her to his family shouldn't have hurt, but it did. Ignoring the sudden wave of emotion, she said, "Maybe you should have changed clothes, worn a suit. Aren't your folks real formal?"

He glanced at his simple black sweater and slacks. "Afraid my own parents will accidentally mistake me for a country preacher or something?"

"No—" Katie gingerly ran a hand along her seat belt strap, uncomfortable with the way it fit. Falling between her breasts, it accentuated them—and Ford definitely seemed to be noticing. "Johnny Cash's double. You know, the man in black."

"But I've got Elvis's hair."

Lush with loose waves, it was thick enough that Katie could grab it in fistfuls. Recalling how it felt, as silken as flax and as soft as flour sifting through her splayed fingers, she suppressed an unwanted shiver of awareness. "Elvis wore white, didn't he?"

Ford nodded. "Only when he was older."

She sobered, thinking of the first night they'd slept together. *I'm too old for you, Katie,* he'd said. *And I'm someone you work with. I've got a whole other lifestyle.* "I think you're the one who said you were old."

He was silent for a moment, then his cheek muscle quivered, and she wondered if he was recalling the context in which he'd said it. "Well, thirty-six isn't old. Not really."

No, every time she looked at him, thirty-six seemed just about perfect. She glanced away, swallowing around a lump that kept forming in her throat. Slowly, in small ways such as this, Ford was trying to shift the ground of their new relationship, to take back the things he'd said about why they'd make a lousy couple. Her heart missed a hopeful beat. "Well, sometimes you think you're old," she reminded. Impulsively, she reached across the seat, pinching a hair from Ford's sweater, her fingers lingering a second too long on the hard, round muscle of his shoulder. She opened her window just enough to toss out the hair. As the wind whisked it away, she noted it was very long, straight and blond. Definitely not Ford's.

He seemed to pick up on the direction of her

thoughts. "Guess the sweater could have used a lint brush."

"You're fine now," she assured him. Except she realized she should have asked about his previous involvements. Whose hair was that, anyway? Knowing she wouldn't like the answer, she decided not to ask just moments before meeting his parents. Still, she was curious. Had she really expected a man as virile as Ford to stay celibate for six months? If he wanted a woman, would it be unfair for her to get upset? Maybe, she thought, since they weren't consummating this marriage; nevertheless, she was wearing Ford's ring and carrying his child. Virile or not, he'd simply have to remain faithful.

Deciding she'd better tell him that later, just to make sure he understood, Katie anxiously fixed her eyes on the view out the window, staring at the ten-foot-high, ivy-covered stone wall they'd been driving alongside for what felt like miles. Every last inch of it circled Carrington property, and she couldn't stop the sudden, nervous puff of breath that she'd been holding back. "I just wish we were on time!"

"It wasn't your fault you had an emergency call, Katie," he reminded her.

Or that her ten-year-old car needed a jump. Or that Ford had come to her rescue like a knight in shining armor wielding jumper cables. They'd started the car just in time to stick themselves in heavy six o'clock traffic. Unfortunately, because of their different work schedules, they'd had to drive the car to Ford's house for the next day.

"Fifteen minutes and we're gone," Ford repeated. "And you do look great, Katie."

She eyed him dubiously, trying not to notice the rush of pleasure brought by the words. "You don't look bad yourself, but seductive, coaxing tones won't work on me, you know."

Her flirtation brought sparkling light to his eyes that dropped appraisingly over the same sage dress she'd worn for their wedding. He smiled. "So, you think I'm seductive?"

Snuggling into the car's plum-colored upholstery, she clasped her hands on the sage raincoat in her lap and shot him a fleeting smile. "Not you. Your *tone.* They're two different..." Her voice trailed off when she noted a far-off break in the stone wall and what looked to be the open front gates to the Carrington mansion. "Anyway," she managed to continue, her anxiety climbing, "I know you're just a sweet-talker by nature." She chuckled. "Amazing you can talk at all, though, since that silver spoon in your mouth takes up so much space."

The unmistakable promise in his voice spiraled through her blood. "So, do I sweet-talk you, Katie?"

She tossed him a glance, the prideful lift of her chin indicating she'd never taken his attentions too seriously, the way some nurses might. "No more than you've probably sweet-talked plenty of women."

He grinned. "Does that bother you?"

Katie laughed. "You really do flatter yourself," she teased, even though she'd definitely devoted too much time to dwelling on Blane Gilcrest. The other woman had spent New Year's Eve with Ford, but had the two been dating seriously? Katie couldn't help but hope not. Blane looked as if she'd stepped from the pages of *Vogue,* and had very long, straight blond hair of the exact sort Katie had just tossed out the window. Catching Ford's gaze, she smirked, "And quit staring at me like that."

He wasn't about to. "Why?"

"It's irritating." *And arousing*.

"What if you're better-looking than the scenery?"

Torn between having fun flirting with him and needing to respect the boundaries she'd laid down after the wedding, Katie lightly said, "C'mon, Ford, cut it out."

His eyes were still sparkling. "You used to like flirting with me."

"Okay," she admitted, her glance playfully meeting his. "It wasn't all I liked, either. There. I said it." Feeling suddenly breathless, she let her eyes drift over the snug fit of his clothes, lingering where fabric hugged hard pectorals and a pancake-flat abdomen and narrow hips. "But things have changed. We're married and pregnant."

"A man can't flirt with his pregnant wife?"

Lord, he didn't give up. "Ford..." Suddenly she was thinking very hard about what she wanted to say. Taking a deep breath, she forged ahead. "If we're ever going to wind up back in bed, Ford, it'll be because we've gotten to know each other better."

There was a long pause. "Do you want to know me better, Katie?"

Her heart hammered. Everything inside her felt tight. "Yeah." Before he could respond, she added, "But honestly, I don't want to talk about this right now. I'm nervous about meeting your folks. I'm just not used to visiting places like this, okay?"

The quick glance he sent her was penetrating, and

it came with a lightning-fast flash of heat. "You haven't even seen the joint yet."

Feeling both relieved and disappointed that she'd managed to change the subject, she repeated, "The joint? You make it sound like a prison. Ford, you grew up in the lap of luxury."

"Maybe. Anyway, they're just people, you know."

"I know they are, but..."

Ford uttered a soft, unexpected curse. "Damn it, I wish you wouldn't feel this way."

Why? Did he really wish she could fit into the Carringtons' world? All at once, the air in the car seemed too thick and warm. "Why?"

"Because I want this to be easier for you, Katie. Regardless of the reasons, we *are* married."

"And having a baby," she added. Instinctively, she reached over the space between them, drew Ford's hand from the wheel and pressed it to her belly. It was too early to feel the life inside her, but the warmth of his hand both calmed her and made her tremble. Vaguely, she knew she was breaking her own rules by initiating the contact, and yet she didn't care. For a second, her palm pressed the back of his hand. They'd made love one special night, and now they were having a baby together. "Sorry," she murmured, sliding his hand to the seat. "But this is a confusing situation. It's not a real marriage, Ford...."

Placing his hand on the steering wheel again, he looked shaken. His tongue flicked out, lightly licking his lips. "Real enough that it's legal, Katie."

Real enough that she'd desperately wanted him in her bed last night. As she'd listened to those insistent hooves pounding, she'd imagined Ford dismounting, his skin warm from the ride. He would come into her room, her bed....

"Katie," he said, his voice low, "we can annul the marriage. Skip meeting my parents. I make a good salary. My business instincts are better than average, so I actually make more from investments. We can work out other financial arrangements. Getting hold of the trust fund isn't necessary. If you think…" Ford paused, uttering another low-voiced curse, his fingers tightening around the steering wheel. "Hell, Katie. I'll go ahead and be blunt. You know how badly I want to sleep with you. And from the way you kiss me, I know you feel the same. But I understand perfectly why, given the circumstances, we shouldn't act on that."

She felt another rush of relief that came in tandem with disappointment. "You do?"

"Sure. But sometimes, when you're so close and you smell so good…well, it's difficult to keep my hands off you. Which is why, if you want to back out now, skip this whole thing…"

Staring through the windshield, she thought of the opportunities they were trying to give their child. Her voice sounded strangely unsteady. "No. We're doing the right thing, Ford. It's for the baby."

His eyes left the windshield, skimming over her with too much male awareness. "Okay, Katie." His abrupt chuckle sounded uncharacteristically nervous. He flashed a quick smile. "There are worse things to live with than a little lust, right?"

Something caught in her throat. "Right." She couldn't help but smile at him. "Thanks."

"For?"

"Being so easy to get along with." A comfortable silence fell—until another rush of nervousness coursed through her. Eyeing the fast-approaching gates, she flipped down the visor mirror and scrutinized her reflection. "I've chewed off my lipstick."

His soft chuckle charmed and unsettled her. "That's what happens when you talk too much about lust."

Sending him another quick smile, she scrounged in a dainty leather pocketbook. The satchel she usually carried was large enough to hold everything from makeup to her horse's bridle. She realized Ford was staring at her. "Hmm?"

"I would have sworn you didn't have a vain bone in your body."

"Guess you're going to find out a lot in six months." As another friendly, tempting smile made the corners of his mouth lift, she added, "Vanity's not a bone, anyway. You should know that. You're a doctor." She glanced from the visor mirror. "And before you wreck and break all our bones, you'd really better keep your eyes on the road."

"Bet that little speech made you feel more in control."

"Men," she returned simply, noticing between smacks and blots that Ford's wayward gaze was drifting over her again. "They never understand."

"We understand better than you think."

"Sorry, but I grew up with three men. I know how they…" *Think.* They'd almost reached the gate. Her heart hammered. She lived in scrubs or sweatpants, so the sage dress was, by far, her best, but now it seemed too understated. Glancing at her watch, she worriedly announced, "We're so late, Ford." By now, Ford's parents would be dressed to the nines, headed to wherever the Carrington Foundation party was being held. As Ford guided the car between the two imposing wrought-iron gates, she inhaled a sharp breath. "I knew the house would be big, but I didn't expect this...." Her eyes were riveted to the brass placard announcing Lincoln's Landing. She felt a heightened sense of dread.

"This isn't a big deal, Katie."

She sent him a long sideways glance. "For all your concern," she said dryly, "this could be a date at a burger joint." A landscaped lawn stretched for seeming miles through the last rays of a Texas winter sunset, and she could see the Carrington mansion gleaming in the distance, stately columns, wraparound verandas and imposing windows.

"I know," Ford joked. "It makes Graceland look like a low-rent condo."

She playfully rolled her eyes. "I bet you've never even been to Graceland, Ford."

"Glad we didn't put any money on that bet," he admitted with a chuckle.

"The lawn looks a little bare," she ventured to add, matching his light tone. "Think they'd like a flock of pink flamingos for Christmas?"

Ford shook his head. "Nope. They're into plastic pinwheels."

"Should have guessed," she murmured, staring toward the center of the circular driveway, where a three-tiered fountain bubbled under blue and pink floodlights. For a second, relief filled her; she imagined Ford had already told his parents everything and that they'd turned on the floodlights in honor of the coming grandchild. He must have meant to surprise her. Then she noted the activity around the entrance. Leaning forward, she peered through the windshield. "What's going on up there?"

Ford raised an eyebrow in surprise. "The foundation party."

Her lips parted. "Foundation party?"

"They have it every year. I told you it was tonight, didn't I?" As if realizing the source of her discomfort, he added, "We're not staying, Katie. I told you that."

"You never said the foundation party was *here*."

"It's always here."

"How was I supposed to know that?" She wasn't a socialite! She'd never been invited to such a place. She'd assumed they were meeting Ford's parents before the party. Now they were close enough to see photographers and uniformed parking attendants. Panicking, she wondered how Ford could have put her in this position. "Turn the car around," she said flatly.

He stared at her. "What?"

"Do it right now. I mean it."

They were already halfway down the drive. "But, Katie…"

What was the man thinking? "I've seen pictures of this event in the papers," she added, her tone more insistent. "In the society column."

His lips had parted in surprise. "So?"

So, only Austin's elite attended, dressed in tuxedos and floor-length gowns that would cost Katie's annual income. "How could such a smart man be so dense?" she fumed.

His tone was dry. "I take it you mean me, Katie?"

Her lips pursed. "I don't see anybody else, do you?" Unfortunately, they'd reached the house. As they circled the fountain, however, she realized they could keep going and head back the way they'd come. Leaning across the seat, she curled her fingers around his arm, then wished she hadn't gotten quite so close as a heady whiff of his cologne sent her senses reeling. "Just keep driving. For me?"

His dark eyes were like lasers on hers. "This'll take fifteen minutes."

"Fifteen minutes!" The hurt she'd felt earlier came back, and unwanted heat rose to her cheeks. It was like flooding water, first overtaking her chin, then her lips, then her cheekbones. By the time it reached her eyebrows, she thought the top of her head might blow clear off. Should she scoot into his lap, take the wheel and get them out of here?

"Fifteen minutes," she repeated. "I know we're just insuring a financial future for our baby, but..." Tears she'd never shed stung her eyes. "Couldn't you have arranged a private dinner with your folks?" she managed to ask as he applied the brake and turned toward her. "Having fifteen minutes to meet my in-laws is...is an insult, Ford." Couldn't he have at least given the illusion that the marriage was real?

Somehow, the softening expression of Ford's eyes only made her feel worse. So did the fact that he cupped his palm around her shoulder, his thumb tracing her collarbone. "Oh, Katie, it was never meant that way."

Maybe not. But now, two uniformed valets on either side of the car swung open the doors and peered inside. One said, "Good evening, Mr. Carrington."

The other grasped Katie's arm and gallantly helped her from the car, saying, "Good evening, ma'am."

And then flashes from countless cameras blinded her.

"FORD, DEAR!" In the crowded, mirrored ballroom, Yvonne Carrington waltzed gracefully past a full orchestra, her gold-sequined gown as blinding as the camera flashes. She smiled through perfect, straight white teeth.

"Mother."

The one word carried a wealth of meaning. Secrets, lies and a world of palpable hurt seemed to radiate from Ford to his mother, and despite her anger at having been manhandled into a room where she already felt unwelcome, Katie sensed dark undercurrents that aroused her curiosity. During the ride here, she'd imagined Ford's family as distant, but not antagonistic. Oh, Yvonne was the picture of social grace, with her smile in place and her warm dark brown eyes sparkling with vitality, but Katie realized instantly she and Ford shouldn't have come.

"Ford, I wish you'd worn a jacket," Yvonne admonished in a hushed undertone, then she draped a gaze down Katie's dress. "Lovely," she pronounced, the smile never leaving her lips, her eyes settling on Katie's matching sage flats.

Oh, the words were right, thought Katie. So was the smile. But both of them knew the dress was all wrong and that Yvonne was silently chastising Ford for bringing Katie. Suddenly, Katie didn't care if Yvonne Carrington was the Queen of England, much less her mother-in-law. She wanted to leave. Determined to be nice, though, she took a deep breath and met the woman's eyes. She had looks as good as Ford's—a gym-hardened body, flat tummy, full lips and golden hair that was done in piled, looped braids. The shimmering gold gown flowed flawlessly down to strappy, barely there sandals.

"Your dress really is gorgeous," Katie said honestly.

*"Really?"* Yvonne returned, letting the word linger, as if Katie had intended to point out Yvonne's insincerity. "Thank you."

Despite the perfect smile and too-polite words, the tension was palpable. "You're welcome," Katie said, realizing that with the party already in swing, they wouldn't be speaking to the Carringtons about the baby tonight. Feeling uncomfortable, Katie gave a brief nod. "Ford," she said, flashing another civil smile at Yvonne, "why don't I just meet you over there?" She pointed toward a distant archway, then added, "A real pleasure, Mrs. Carrington."

Yvonne smiled back. "The same." She turned toward Ford, smiling and waving at some other guests. "I wish you'd worn a suit," she continued as if Katie had never been present. "You know what this party means to your father."

"Katie, hold on," Ford said. "Mother, I told you we were coming. We just need a minute of your time."

Katie could only shake her head. What kind of family talked like this? And what was the real cause of the tension between Ford and his mother? "Really, Ford," Katie murmured, this time stepping away, "I'll meet you over there."

Wincing as she wended through a sea of designer gowns, Katie wished she hadn't worn flats. Given the stilettos surrounding her, she was a good four inches shorter than everyone else and she felt positively dwarfed. The farther she moved away from Ford, the more intimidated she became, too. *A real pleasure,* she thought, the words she'd spoken to Yvonne playing in her head.

"Right," she whispered. Ford hadn't even managed to introduce her to her new mother-in-law. All day, this meeting had been on Katie's mind, but now nothing was to come of it. Worse, that meant they'd have to meet with the Carringtons another time, and if Katie had had any doubts about how they'd welcome their son's wife, she now knew. Ford had been well aware of how his mother would react, too. Katie was sure of it. Not wearing a suit and bringing her here had been intentional—if unconscious—provocations.

Moving at a faster clip, Katie kept her gaze locked on the archway she'd indicated to Ford. A microphone and speakers were positioned in front of it, so that David Carrington could announce the annual monetary awards given out by the foundation. Glancing around, Katie recognized many newsworthy faces, though not all the people were well-heeled, she realized. They were probably working stiffs like Katie, people hoping to be awarded charitable contributions, so that they could fund health-related projects in which they deeply believed. Well, Katie conceded, there was no denying that the Carringtons contributed to worthy causes in Austin. They couldn't be all bad.

She had almost made it to the archway when gridlock set in, and she found herself smushed against a lace-covered buffet table, momentarily powerless except to clutch her raincoat and stare at the towering ice sculptures. Artfully fashioned mermaids and leaping fish peered from pedestals at trays of smoked salmon and cut crystal dishes of caviar and fruit. Katie had about decided Yvonne must have personally dragged both oceans to find so many jumbo shrimp, when a cultured, husky voice said, "I don't believe we've met. I'm a close friend of Ford Carrington's. I saw you two come in together." With that, a smiling Blane Gilcrest crunched two bleached-white teeth into a cracker piled high with caviar. She was so tall that Katie had to lean back to meet her gaze.

Round, almost violet eyes stared back. "I'm Blane Gilcrest," she repeated. "Ford's friend."

*I'm Katie Topper Carrington, Ford's wife.*

Knowing it wasn't in her best interest to announce that at the moment, especially since Blane was obviously marking her territory with Ford, Katie found herself studying the straight, white-blond hair that lovingly caressed Blane's flawless neck, creamy sloping jaw and high cheekbones. Diamond-studded spaghetti straps hooked over Blane's smooth tanned shoulders, holding up a low-cut, slinky black gown. If good looks were what men sought in women, Ford could not have done better.

"Blane. Uh…I've seen your picture in the papers." There. That seemed politic, even flattering. Unable to resist the urge, Katie lifted a hand and smoothed her hair, only to find that the curls were frizzed at the ends. Vaguely, she realized four-inch heels still wouldn't bring her gaze level with Blane's shoulders.

"My picture... Ah." Blane smiled. "Probably with Ford in the society columns." Her smile broadened. "He photographs so well, don't you think?"

Unfortunately, Blane possessed about as much sincerity as Ford's mother. She appeared to be furious Ford wasn't her date tonight, and despite her effort at conversation, she seemed to want to know why he'd come here with Katie. When her eyes flickered over Katie's dress, a barely discernible hint of satisfaction appeared. Obviously, if Ford had meant this as a date, Blane seemed to be thinking, he and Katie would have dressed appropriately.

It was probably the truth. That's what hurt. "He's very good-looking," Katie agreed.

Blane's low voice blended into the orchestral music, forcing Katie to lean closer to hear. "Oh," Blane said. "Aren't you the nurse from Maitland Maternity? The one Ford calls Carrot Top? It's seemed so gruelling over there lately. Ford's working such long hours...."

Or so he told you, Katie thought wickedly.

"Were you two working late tonight?"

*No. We left from the home we now share.* Given the things she was tempted to say, there was no doubt in Katie's mind that she was feeling a twinge of jealousy. "No," she said simply. "We didn't."

Blane eyed her a long moment. "Well, it was nice of him to bring you." She glanced around. "Isn't everything fabulous? Yvonne throws a great party."

The tone implied Katie had never been anywhere nearly as nice—and made her feel as if she might implode. "It's a nurse from the hospital," Blane continued, playfully snagging the arm of a girlfriend who looked just as tall and intimidating. "She was stargazing at the buffet."

*Stargazing.* "Looking for some Buffalo wings and a long-neck beer," Katie assured her dryly, her eyes locking with Blane's.

When Blane and the other woman laughed, the sound seemed delicate and deadly, like broken, tinkling glass. How could Ford have brought her here? Katie wondered, staring at the other two women. Whatever his feelings for Blane, the woman obviously thought she and Ford were a couple.

Just as Katie saw an opening, murmured an excuse and turned away, Ford appeared. "There you are!"

Blane quickly grabbed his arm. "Your dad's about ready to make the announcements, and I said I'd introduce him. But I haven't seen you for so long, Ford! Why don't we dance?" Ford protested, but her perky voice bubbled with laughter. "Make room, everybody. Ford and I are headed for the dance floor!"

Enough people stepped back that Ford would appear rude if he refused. Her eye catching Katie's, Yvonne smiled placidly. Knowing it was the right thing to do, Katie nodded, sending Ford a look of understanding. Why embarrass Blane and make things worse than they already were?

Without waiting to see what happened, Katie turned and pushed through the crowd, her eyes fixed on the mirrored wall in front of her and the microphone near the archway. She was almost there when Ford appeared behind her, reflected in the mirrors. She watched as he glided onto the dance floor. He didn't look entirely happy about dancing with Blane, but he waltzed before the orchestra with the grace of

Fred Astaire, thoroughly in his element with a beautiful woman draped over his arm.

Katie's heart ached. It took years to learn to dance like that, and Ford belonged with a woman who knew how. *Quit doing this to yourself, Katie!* Their marriage was a financial arrangement, nothing more, and if she'd wanted proof, it was right there on the dance floor. Maybe that's why she'd encouraged it, just to remind herself.

Reaching the makeshift stage, she almost toppled the microphone. As she righted the stand, she heaved a sigh, put on her raincoat so she wouldn't have to carry it, then continued down a dark-paneled hallway that was lined with cocktail-sipping guests. Overhearing some rumblings about the foundation being in financial trouble, she frowned. Then someone said, "We'd better go in. After the glamorous couple dances, I bet David'll make the announcements."

*The glamorous couple.*

She grimaced as the words knifed into her. She was about to duck inside a bathroom when a man thrust a champagne flute into her hand. Oblivious of Katie's shock, he said, "I asked for champagne but this is sparkling apple juice. Could you get me another?" Then, looking askance at Katie's coat, he added, "You do work here, don't you?"

She stared a long moment at the man, then took a healthy swallow from the drink he'd handed her and said, "Bottoms up. I think I just quit."

He was still gaping when Blane's voice came over the microphone. "Welcome to the annual Carrington Foundation party!"

"Glad to be here," Katie whispered, turning and

pushing open the bathroom door. She felt about as welcome as a stray dog. Not that she really blamed Ford's mother. From Yvonne's point of view, her son had crashed a fancy party, inappropriately dressed and with an unsuitable date. Katie glanced around, taking in the French moldings, plush red carpet and gold-lined fluted sink basin as she seated herself at a makeup vanity. *"Bonjour,"* she said to her reflection, trying to boost her spirits with the only French word she knew. Then she realized she was shaking with anger. Despite her graciousness, she really didn't want Ford dancing with Blane. Beyond the door, Katie could hear the guests settling down, their chatter subsiding to whispers.

"Can we have quiet please?" Blane asked, sounding so breathless from dancing that Katie's heart sank. Why couldn't she and Ford be left alone right now? As she'd admitted in the car, she wanted them to get to know each other. Ford seemed to want that, too. Oh, she had no illusions, but maybe some lasting feelings could develop, separate from those about the baby they shared.

"As so many of you know," Blane continued, "in addition to his long-term involvement with the Gilcrest Endowment for the Sciences, my father, Gil Gilcrest, is the attorney for the Carrington Foundation. I, too, have come to share an interest in the organization."

An interest in Ford was more like it, Katie thought as she listened to Blane ramble about a proposed merger between the Gilcrest Endowment and the Carrington Foundation.

"And now…" A drumroll sounded from the orchestra. "David Carrington."

"Hello there, everybody."

Ford's voice was deeper than his father's, but David's long, ambling cadences were the same. "As you know," he continued in a cultured drawl, "we usually announce the yearly allocations now. Tonight, we're sorry to disappoint you. Due to the number of interesting proposals, selection has been tougher than usual, and no final decisions have yet been reached. We'll be announcing them soon, though, and you'll be apprised of that date."

Discontented rumblings followed, and Katie frowned. Austin's social elite wouldn't care if the awards weren't made—they wouldn't be affected— but didn't Ford's father know the recipients were waiting on pins and needles? As a medical professional, Katie had followed the Carrington Foundation for years, and there'd never been a delay in announcing allocations. What could have happened?

"It's not any of your business," she mouthed. She wasn't a Carrington, not really. She might be married to Ford, but she didn't love him, right?

The eyes staring at her in the mirror said differently. So did her heart. Her fingers curled around the flute of sparkling juice again. "Everybody here thinks you're a barmaid, Katie," she whispered.

*I've got to get out of here.*

Rising, glass in hand, she pushed through the door, thinking she could live ten lifetimes without seeing Ford again, if only to punish him for bringing her here. His father was just leaving the microphone. "Again we'll invite you once the selections have been made," David Carrington was saying. "Meantime, eat, drink and be merry."

"Here," Katie said, handing her glass to the man who'd given her the juice in the first place. "And thanks. I needed that."

Pausing only long enough to enjoy his curious expression, she headed for the door. Maybe she should take Ford up on the offer he'd made in the car. No one knew about their marriage, so maybe they should annul it as he'd suggested. Love made babies grow, not money, and she'd been a fool to be sucked into this charade. She'd told him she wanted to know him better, but she was sure she was going to get hurt.

In fact, she already felt hurt. Damn it, why couldn't she be crazy about some down-to-earth guy who'd want to raise their kids on a little spread in the country?

She speeded up, her strides lengthening purposefully as she neared the archway. Just a few more steps and she'd be out of here. Yes, she should change her mind and get an annulment. Ford would agree. She'd never have to know his parents. Feeling better, Katie told herself she didn't care if the car was parked in Mexico. Right about now, she could walk home if she had to. She was a resourceful girl. Remembering the valet parking, she gave a sigh of relief. The keys were probably still in Ford's car. *I'll drive. He can walk.* She squelched a flash of him catching a ride home with Blane, and as if on cue, she swiftly rounded the archway and nearly ran into the woman.

"Where are you headed so fast?" the attractive blonde asked lightly. "Aren't you having a good time?"

Obviously, Blane couldn't have been happier to see Katie leaving. "I just need a little air," Katie lied, not stopping but tossing the words over her shoulder.

"If you stay," Blane called out, "I'm sure Ford's looking for another dance partner."

The words were out before she thought them through. "My husband does love to dance."

Blane stopped in her tracks, looking stunned. "Husband?"

Katie could have kicked herself. What had come over her? Feeling her back hit something tall and solid, she gasped, reaching around and swiping the air. Just as she caught the microphone stand, her ankle twisted. Blane had followed her. "Did you just say Ford Carrington is your husband?"

"Yes." Katie lurched to one side, righted herself, then stood very still, her lips parting and her heart filling with dread. Blane's words had broadcast to a large, now very silent crowd, and Yvonne and David Carrington weren't a foot away.

Katie realized she was still gripping the microphone, her wedding ring catching the light. "Married and pregnant," she whispered, knowing there was no way to save the situation.

And then, as calmly as she could, she managed a slight smile, turned on her sage green flats and made a beeline across the room, feeling sure she'd die from sheer mortification.

She was nearly at the door when a man's voice shouted, "Bravo, Carrot Top!"

## CHAPTER FIVE

FORD STARED through the windshield at the crowd milling inside the ballroom—no doubt the place was still alive with gossip. He smiled, his breath clouding the air as he replayed Katie's grand exit in his mind. God only knew what his parents were thinking now. Or Katie. She looked lost in thought, her open raincoat flapping as she wended her way through the darkened parking area behind the house, circling limousines and luxury cars with her head down, shoulders hunched and hands fisted. Every now and again she shook her head as if she was having an argument with herself, her petite, curvy body moving at a fast clip. Watching her in the rearview mirror, he recalled how she'd brought his hand to her belly on the drive here, how her body warmth had seeped through her dress to his palm. "She's having my baby," he whispered, as if saying it would make it seem more real.

Her eyes lighted on his car, and within seconds, she flung open the driver's door. The dome light snapped on, and her right hand was already fumbling for the keys in the ignition as she swung inside, her gaze focused on the house in the distance. When her rear landed in a man's lap, not the seat, she gave a startled jerk. "Ford!" Grasping the steering wheel so she could turn to face him, she accidentally depressed the horn.

Chuckling softly, he said, "Calm down. We don't need to attract attention."

Katie shook her head, sounding miserable. "That's all we seem to be doing this evening." As she twisted further, he shifted his weight so her knees hooked over his thighs, her legs dangled beside his. Rustling his hands under her coat, he wrapped his arms around her waist, then wished she hadn't stiffened as if she might protest. A second later, she relaxed. "What are you doing here, anyway, Ford?"

"Making sure you don't steal my car," he said, taking the risk of sliding a hand downward, molding it over the warm curve of her hip. "Don't you know that would have been grand theft auto?"

She offered the slightest of smiles, trying not to appear overly aware of the fact that she'd landed in his embrace. "The way you looked out for me at that party, Ford," she said, glancing toward the ballroom windows, "you deserve punishment." She shook her head. "The electric chair, maybe. No, forget that. It's too modern and humane. Let's just draw and quarter you."

He thought of the way Blane accidentally announced their marriage over the microphone. "Things seem that dire to you, huh?"

An annoyed toss of her head made red-gold tendrils fly around her face, glinting even more than her eyes, which shone under the dome light like hot sun on emerald chrome. "I thought it over in there," she said seriously, glancing at him from her perch on his lap. "And maybe..." She looked away. "Maybe you were right earlier. We could annul this marriage. Just tell your folks that it was a bad joke."

Feeling as if someone had kicked him in the chest, Ford realized he wanted this marriage in ways he was still struggling to understand. The wind whooshed out of him, and his words sounded strained. "On the drive over, I thought you said you wanted us to get to know each other."

Her eyes settled on his, their honest, worried expression making his heart stutter. A sage shoe skated toward the open car door, and the movement hiked her dress hem. Suddenly, he was focused on the nearness of her pursed lips and the warmth of their mingling breath. "Katie," he murmured. "C'mon, do you really want to end things? What are you saying?"

"Just that what we're doing is crazy."

Marrying Katie was feeling less crazy to him by the minute. Finding one of her hands, he turned it in his, and as he rubbed his thumb into the warm, cushiony center of a palm, her sharp, barely audible intake of breath went through him as surely as if he'd inhaled it himself. His eyes roved over her face, taking in her flushed scarlet cheeks, and his tongue suddenly felt too thick for his mouth. "C'mon, Katie. It's not that crazy."

Looking uncertain, she stared toward the ballroom again. "I'm so embarrassed about what happened in there," she finally said. "I didn't mean for your parents to find out that way. But then Blane stepped up to the microphone...."

"I saw." Against the heel of his palm, he could feel the insistent throbbing pulse at her wrist; it wreaked havoc with his senses, making heat flood his groin. He hadn't felt this excited by a woman for a long time. Exactly three months. Taking a deep breath, he lifted a hand and brushed a thumb over her lips, feeling the smooth glaze of bronze lipstick. With quiet desperation, he wanted to kiss it off her mouth.

"Ford," she murmured in faint protest.

"You said you wanted to get to know me better," he returned simply. When she didn't say anything, he added, "My parents needed to find out one way or another. Don't worry. I'll call first thing tomorrow and smooth things over."

She stared at him a long moment, looking undecided, the pulse in her throat ticking. "Since the first time I saw you, I wanted to get to know you," she admitted, her soft drawl reminding him of things that were dark and smoky, both candy-sweet and yet forbidden. "I never imagined things could wind up like this, though."

His eyes held hers, the idea of her interest in him doing funny things to his heart. "You wanted to get to know me?"

She swallowed hard. "Yeah."

He frowned. "Then why do you always leave after work?"

She shrugged, glancing away. "At first I tried talking to you outside the OR…"

Had she? He thought back. Megan Maitland had introduced them, but the memory was sketchy. Cute, he'd thought of Katie. Easy smile. Sparkling wisdom in her emerald eyes. Her skin radiating with the bright glow of healthy sexuality. But had he really thought that then? Or was it only now? Lifting a finger, he swept it lightly against her cheek, brushing back a lock of hair that burned like fire where light touched it. "Wish you'd tried harder," he said throatily.

A soft flush suffused her cheeks. "Maybe it's not that easy to get your attention."

Looking at her, he could only shake the head he now knew he should have examined. How had he worked with her for so long and never tried to date her? "I don't know how I could have missed you, Katie." His gaze followed hers, settling where she was still staring at the ballroom. "I can't tell you how many times you've made my day better."

She nodded. "I like working with you, too."

"And now we're married," he murmured. "And pregnant."

A small sigh escaped her. "Strange, huh?"

He nodded. "Very." He watched her a long, silent moment—his eyes on hers, hers on the ballroom. Unbidden, their kiss in the church came back to him, and he felt the sizzling heat, the deep pressure, the sweet taste. His stomach fluttered, his groin tightened, and his eyes dropped to her lips. If he kissed her again right now, he knew, everything would change. Getting to know a woman better when you were already married to her was a complicated proposition, especially if she was having your child. How close could he and Katie get before they were in a real marriage? And how must his life look to her? he wondered, shifting his gaze over the huge imposing house where he'd spent a childhood he'd sooner forget. He tried to see the place through her eyes. "Believe it or not, Katie," he found himself saying, turning solemn and feeling he was reading her mind, "there's…a lot in life I haven't gotten."

She turned toward him, the expression in her green eyes touching him in a place he hadn't known existed until now. "Like what?"

Instead of answering her, he said, "I like your eyes."

Her smile deepened. "Why?"

He tilted his head and considered, though he already knew. "They're curious. Like you really *do* want to get to know me."

She frowned. "Of course I want to."

He pondered that. "I'm not sure many people have, Katie. At least not the real me."

"The real you? As opposed to?" The soft, sweet, dubious sound she made fell between a sigh and a chuckle.

"As opposed to a Carrington." His voice lowered, turning almost hoarse. "When I was a kid, I always felt paraded out in front of guests on nights like tonight. Every year, the foundation party would roll around, and someone, a nanny usually, would dress me up and bring me down to say good-night."

"And that made you feel as if people didn't want to get to know you?"

He shrugged. "Yeah." Moments after saying good-night, he'd be back upstairs, still warmed by the glow that always seemed to surround his parents, having experienced just five fleeting minutes of perfection before his bedroom light was extinguished.

Katie was frowning, her sparse red brows knitted and a hint of confusion in her eyes as she glanced between him and the house. "What didn't you have when you were growing up?"

"Love, Katie. I didn't feel I got enough of that."

His eyes lifted to hers. "And I guess I'm worried," he admitted, resting a hand on the steering wheel and blowing out a sigh. "My parents and I don't get along. You could tell that much. Which means I don't know the first thing about being a good father."

Color seeped into her cheeks, and she looked so gorgeous that he couldn't help but lift his hand from the wheel again; slowly, he stroked his knuckles along the underside of a silken jaw, barely able to believe what was happening between them, that he was touching her so easily and familiarly.

"You'll be a great dad," she defended, her flush deepening at his touch. "You're..." Shrugging, she shook her head as if she didn't know where to begin. "So reliable. So patient. So funny."

Chewing the inside of his cheek thoughtfully, he let his knuckles drop, the backs of his fingers touching her neck, which felt damp from the dewy night. A rush of fury at his parents coursed through him as he stared at Lincoln's Landing again. Living in that house had been so painful that he'd never even considered having a child of his own before now. "I wish we'd had the kind of warm family life you seem to have."

"You're going to be a great dad," Katie repeated.

*Dad.* Hearing the word made his gut clench. "Thanks for the vote of confidence, Katie. Coming from you, it means a lot."

She lifted an eyebrow. "It does?"

He nodded. "I know it was an accident, but if I'd been looking, there's no other woman I'd want more to be the mother of my child."

Her voice caught. "You mean it?"

He shrugged. "Because of the way we've worked together." He'd helped her save so many lives, watched her calm distraught parents whose loved child was going into surgery, and smile at newborns with a sheen of tears glossing her eyes.

"No one's opinion could mean more to me," she assured him. As she spoke, a deep inhalation drew her musky, warm scent into his lungs. Feeling uncomfortable with the revelations and oddly exposed, Ford smiled, changing the subject. "Don't think I've ever smelled the perfume you're wearing, Katie."

She laughed softly, her teasing voice sending a ripple of awareness through him. "Has anything that costs less than a hundred dollars an ounce ever flared those patrician nostrils of yours?"

He grinned back. "Maybe not. What is it, anyway?"

Playful lights warmed her eyes. "You're getting awfully personal."

As if the snug way she fit in his lap wasn't personal. "Very," he agreed, his eyes capturing hers, the rest of him reveling in the feel of her. "C'mon, what is it?"

"The sixty-four-thousand-dollar question." Looking flattered, she added, "Soap and water."

"And you," he couldn't help but say huskily. "It's the smell of you, Katie." As he inhaled another deep breath of naturally aroused woman, wide bands tightened around his chest, and his throat became as dry as a Texas drought. "Katie," he repeated, his voice catching with need, his hands gripping her hips, holding her in place. "Do you know you're where I've wanted you all night?'' *Where I've dreamed of you for the last three months?*

She stared at her feet, her eyes glittering like wet chiseled stones. Leaning his head against the headrest, he watched her, his skin prickling with heat when he noticed how her dress had twisted, the already deep V neck revealing a hint of a lace bra, the beginning swell of her breasts and sumptuous cleavage. Just looking at her, he could barely believe his good fortune. Maybe love, which had always seemed to elude him, was as close as the woman in his lap.

Katie looked a tad wary, as if realizing she was about to be kissed, which she was. She licked her lips nervously. ''Look, Ford,'' she began. ''I'm scared you're developing feelings that have more to do with the baby than me. It's the only thing that makes me feel we shouldn't...''

*Get to know each other better.* Words she'd previously spoken hung in the air. ''You're having my baby, Katie,'' he returned, his voice a low rumble. ''I can't begin to tell you what that means to me. The news got my attention, but even if you weren't pregnant, I'd want to be exactly where we are right now.''

She took a deep breath, glancing around, taking in the quiet, dark night outside, then the chilly, illuminated interior of the car. When she spoke, her voice was so low he strained closer to hear it. ''What about Blane?''

The question took him by surprise. ''Blane? What about her?''

''What's your relationship?''

There wasn't one. ''We dated casually.'' Dated. Past tense. Feeling taken aback, he added, ''I...mean to respect our wedding vows, if that's what you're worried about, Katie.'' Of course, with her in his lap, going six months without sex didn't seem even remotely possible.

''We never discussed it. And we should have. I...just wondered. Your mother really seems to like Blane.''

Lifting a hand, he brushed another fallen curl from her forehead. ''It's my life, Carrot Top, not theirs.'' He shrugged. ''I guess my parents would have liked for me and Blane to get together, mostly because her father's our attorney. Also, the Gilcrest Endowment is considering jointly funding projects with the foundation, since the foundation's having money problems right now.''

Katie distractedly wove her fingers through her hair. ''You're angry about your parents wanting you to go out with Blane?''

''I wish they could accept me on another level,'' he explained. ''That's all. They should want me to have a woman who's right for me, not them.'' When Katie looked vaguely disturbed, he added, ''Blane could never be right, Katie.'' But could Katie? Just wondering made his chest tighten.

''And the foundation?'' she asked. ''It's having money trouble? I heard something to that effect in the hallway at the party.''

His voice hardened. ''I steer clear of the foundation's business.''

''Isn't it a family endeavor?''

A grunt of derision escaped him. ''You were in there, Katie. My parents barely spoke to me. We're not close. And I have no idea how I'd even go about getting to know them better. I don't even come to this annual bash. There are a lot of nice people in there. I admit that. But others are so phony. Superficial. You're in, you're out. You're up, you're down. Never coasting. So, you're right. Maybe I don't care. What's to care about?"

"The foundation's so worthwhile," Katie returned, looking increasingly worried. "And they're your family, Ford."

He was surprised. "Now you sound upset."

She looked upset, too. She pursed her lips and crossed her arms, but the schoolmarm's stance only raised her breasts, and when he dragged his eyes down the front of her, he remembered the hot September night they'd shared three months ago, how she'd tugged the T-shirt over her head and bared herself to him. Releasing a frustrated sigh of longing, he glanced toward the house again.

"We don't get to pick our family members," Katie was saying. "We have to get along with them."

Ignoring a slow pull of arousal, he said, "Family means that much to you, huh?" When she nodded, he continued, "Well, your brothers are great, and I can tell you love your dad."

"No matter what, I'd be in their lives," she agreed. "Even if things weren't easy, we'd pull together." Clasping her hands in her lap, she worried her thumbs. "Which is why I feel so guilty about not telling my papa we're married."

"We will. As soon as he gets back."

"It won't be much longer, but maybe we should just drive over to Dallas and tell him. It's not that far away."

"I say we wait," said Ford. "Just as we planned. Tell him on his own turf. It'll be better if he's here. We can spend time with him then. Have dinner. Maybe go trail riding. Jem and Gary said he likes to do that."

Ford wasn't sure, but he could swear hopefulness came into her gaze. "You really want to get to know my papa?"

Eyeing Katie, he nodded. "Yeah." Divorced parents wouldn't make for the best family, he found himself thinking, his eyes flickering over her face. Who knew? Maybe he'd hit it off with her papa, the way he had with her brothers. With the baby, maybe he could learn to open his heart a little. With Katie, too. Maybe this could turn into the real thing, something that could last.

She was still worrying her crossed thumbs. "Were you sleeping with Blane, Ford?"

The question came out of the blue, catching him off guard. Wincing, he thought of the blond hair Katie had pulled off his sweater earlier. More likely, it was Essie's, the maid's, not Blane's. "No, Katie. I never have. Like I said, it would have been convenient if we hit it off. I guess Blane hoped...."

"But you were with her on New Year's."

Somehow he liked that Katie cared enough to remember and ask him about it. "Yeah. But like I said, it was a casual date."

"She seemed to believe you were involved."

He shrugged. "But we're not. And looks can be deceiving. She's skin deep. She could be chasing someone else tomorrow." Glancing around, Ford leaned over, pulling the door handle. As the door shut and the dome light snapped out, he reached around Katie and turned the key in the ignition. "Just running the heater," he explained, his voice sounding raspier than he'd intended.

Over the steady hum of the heater came the quick rustling of her coat. The way she wrapped it around her, he guessed she knew he'd been reacting to the way her chest looked—the knit fabric tight against sloping mounds, her nipples beading because she was chilled from the night. He glanced upward, his heart missing a beat. His eyes traced a lock of hair that was wrapped around the shell of a delicate ear, then landed on the twinkling diamond at the top. In a million years, he'd never have imagined he'd wind up married to Katie Topper or be sitting here like this, with her pregnant and snuggled in his lap. Suddenly, the air felt too warm, not from the heater but from the fact that she made his internal thermostat rise.

"What's going on between you and your mother?" she asked, the faint huskiness of her voice curling through him. "There was so much tension in there."

He was used to it, so he'd barely noticed. "Unlike with your brothers, huh?" he said, avoiding the subject out of habit. "I really do like them, Katie."

Her voice hitched. "You do?" Shifting her weight, she settled further into him, her knees tightening where they were hooked over his thigh.

He nodded. "Yeah. I liked being at your farm." More words were on the tip of his tongue, about the brother he'd lost, but Ford held them back.

"The tension in there got to me," she continued, staring at the ballroom again, her expression pensive. "And I guess, if I'm honest, I don't appreciate being brought here like this.'' She bit her lower lip. ''I...I felt used, Ford.''

Something knifed into him. ''Used? Katie, I didn't...''

''Yes, you did,'' she insisted, her face paling slightly. ''You don't get along with your folks, and you...''

''Katie,'' he returned levelly, realizing again as he spoke how much her good opinion of him mattered. ''I'd never want to see you flounder.'' He couldn't believe she'd think so. ''Believe me,'' he reiterated. ''Never.''

''No.'' She shook her head thoughtfully. ''But you didn't mind seeing your parents in a jam. That's why you yelled 'bravo.' I heard you. By having them find out about our marriage and the baby in such a public way...'' She blew out a quick, audible breath. ''I played right into your hands, Ford.''

Uttering a soft curse, he glided a hand swiftly upward, tracing her spine. ''There's some truth in what you're saying. I'm not proud of it, but I'll admit it. Still, I wouldn't hurt you, Katie. C'mon. We've worked together a long time. You know me better than that. It's just...it's complex.''

''Families always are. That doesn't mean it was fair to lead me into a situation where I was in the dark. Especially since...since I guess we'll be seeing your parents again.''

''No, we won't. We don't have to. The trust for the baby can be handled through lawyers.''

''No,'' she said decisively, her jaw setting with determination. ''Your parents will want to care for this baby.''

He offered a derisive grunt. Clearly, Katie couldn't imagine their child not enjoying the benefits of an extended family. "Nice idea, but I can't imagine it. Honestly, Katie, I never felt they cared that much for me, so the baby…"

"Maybe this baby will make things different, Ford. Bring you all together again."

Ford knew it wouldn't, but the words made his heart do a flip-flop anyway. "That'd be nice," he admitted, staring at Lincoln's Landing. Huge and white, the house gleamed in the night. He loved it, hated it. Right now, he could almost hear the heavy front door closing behind him, how the gurgling water sounded as it cascaded down through the tiered basins of the fountain before being recycled. How many times had he left here, vowing not to return—only to find himself back once more? Maybe the past was like the endlessly recycled water in the fountain. It kept coming back.

Katie tried to scoot across him, intending to move into the passenger seat, but the flex of his fingers stayed her. Resting a hand on her belly, he gently smoothed the fabric, imagining the smoothness of her skin beneath, feeling warmth because he knew the baby was there. "Stay," he said simply.

"Ford…" She sounded worried, her eyes riveted on the house. "What aren't you telling me?"

His gaze traveled over the upstairs windows of the house, most of which were in darkness. He knew each room down to the smallest details: an irregular knot of oak on his closet door; a cigarette burn on the grand piano that was hidden by sheet music; a barely discernible ink stain on the Oriental rug in his father's study. Yeah, he thought. Lincoln's Landing was a house that kept its flaws well hidden. Outsiders often sensed something was wrong, though, just as Katie had.

He wished she wasn't quite so perceptive, and yet he wanted to share himself with her. Unlike Blane and so many other women he'd known, Katie could listen. He felt the touch of her hand as she gingerly placed it on the headrest, her fingers trailing lightly into his hair. His gaze shifted, taking in the dark night, the vast array of stars; the crowds visible through the ballroom windows. Then Katie. He pointed upward. "See that light?"

Ducking, she peered through the windshield. "In the upstairs window?"

He nodded. "That was my little brother's room."

Frowning, she said, "Thought you were an only child."

He shook his head. "No. And back there..."

Her weight shifted in his lap and he sighed at the pressure as she glanced over the headrest, through the back window. "Looks like stables." Her frown deepened. "You love horses."

"Yeah," he murmured, his mind in the past, recalling the brother who hadn't lived past the age of three, whose life had been taken far too soon. "I felt like it was my fault," he said, glad that Katie let him run a thumb down the liquid-soft skin of her cheek. "I was ten. I loved horses then, still do. I didn't know anything about danger, though. You know how it is when you're a kid." He forced a smile. "Life's full of adventure."

Looking concerned, Katie nodded. "Sure. You've got no real sense of consequences."

"My kid brother was three. Lincoln was his name."

She sucked in a breath. "The brass plaque on the front gate said Lincoln's Landing. This place is named for him?"

He should have known she'd guess. "Yeah. At the funeral, my father said something about Lincoln's soul always floating in the air. Dad said this would always be Lincoln's home, and that the light would stay on in case he wanted to land here again." Ford shook his head ruefully. "He was the greatest kid. Three, and into everything. He'd follow me everywhere, like a puppy. I was older, seven when he was born, so he really looked up to me." He shrugged. "Mother was thirty when I came along, and thirty-seven when she had Lincoln. Now she's sixty-six. My father's older.... Realizing his voice had trailed off, he added, "So, after what happened to Lincoln, they felt they were too old to have any more kids."

Against his side, Ford could feel Katie's body tense; her eyes narrowed with concern. He drew a deep breath. "Lincoln wasn't allowed to go to the stables with me, but one day when our nanny wasn't around—she was in my father's study discussing something—I took him there with me so he could pet the horses. I put him down for a minute and went to get some grain so he could feed them."

Katie's sharp intake of breath was audible. "He got into one of the stalls?"

Air squeezed from Ford's chest as if it had happened yesterday. "A mare kicked him. He was still breathing when I found him.'' Reliving the moment, Ford could still hear the high, piercing scream that was suddenly cut short. He bit back a curse and shook his head. ''Since then, I've seen death so many times, I can't count them all, Katie. You know that.'' She'd been in surgery with him often enough. ''I wish I could say…that it came instantly.''

Katie stroked his hair, offering comfort. ''It didn't?''

He shook his head, still staring at his house. ''Later, I found out his trachea was nearly crushed. I grabbed him, put him on the horse—the same damn horse that had kicked him—and galloped to the house. But by then…''

''I'm sorry, Ford.''

''Somewhere on the ride…'' Taking a deep breath, Ford shrugged. ''Later, I wished I'd stopped riding, but keeping him still wouldn't have helped. Now I'd know how to save him.''

''Only a seasoned doctor could have,'' she murmured.

''I panicked. I was trying to get to the phone, to call an ambulance. I thought maybe my father could do something for him.''

''You think your parents blamed you?''

Working in medicine, Katie had seen that kind of reaction, as had Ford. ''Yeah…yeah, I think they did, Katie.'' Glancing at the house, he shook his head. ''But I don't know. I know it's not really my fault, just unfortunate circumstances. For a couple of years after that, I couldn't even look at a horse, but slowly I started riding again. With my parents, it wasn't so easy. I'd been told never to take him down there.

Maybe I blamed myself and just wouldn't let them get close to me after that. Maybe I was afraid I'd hurt them even more, somehow. Anyway, they're not naturally affectionate people, so it's hard to say. It was so many years ago.''

Katie's eyes offered more compassion than he'd ever known. "How long?"

"Twenty-six years." As he stared at the light in Lincoln's window, he found it hard to believe so much time had passed. He could hear his brother's laughter, see his dark eyes and golden hair that was so like their mother's. "It nearly killed my mother. She was really bitter after that. I didn't know what to do, what to say, how to fix things.''

"Your father?''

"He threw himself into his work at Texas General, and then, after my grandfather died, he spent the rest of his time working with the foundation.''

"And you became a doctor.''

He nodded, knowing she'd discovered what motivated him. "I wanted to go into business. By the time I was ten, I knew the family profession wasn't for me." Silence said the rest. No other child had been available to carry on the Carrington legacy, and every child Ford saved now was, in some way, his brother.

"But you're such a good doctor, Ford. The best.''

His lips twisted into a smile that didn't meet his eyes. "Not bad. But better at business. Anyway, I've grown to like it." His smile became more genuine. "I met this girl where I work....''

Her lips curled at the edges. "You did?''

"Her name's Katie." And she was looking at him with such real understanding that his heart swelled.

"You're a good person, Carrot Top. Probably better than you know." He stared at the house again. Joy had once filled it. After Lincoln died, Ford had sometimes felt as if the house were actually growing, the laughter inside it becoming fainter, echoing in rooms that were even larger and emptier. "If only I hadn't gone to the stables that morning, Katie."

"I'm sorry," she said once more.

"Me, too." He became aware of her again, of how much he wanted her, of how much he needed this closeness now and of how much he'd always needed it. It was too soon to tell her what he felt, but he did so with a gesture, slowly rubbing his hand over her back, then upward again, into her hair, exerting just enough pressure to bring her nearer, to feel her breasts cushioning his chest. She slipped her arms around his neck.

Nothing was said. Only the heater's hum and their quiet breathing intruded on the silence as he cupped her neck and tilted her head back, exposing the soft cylinder of skin, his dark gaze flickering from her eyes to lips she'd licked to dampness. His mouth settled then, the kiss slow, firm and hot. Her lips parted, just a fraction at first, then opening wider in invitation, and when their tongues meshed, he knew he'd never forget the depth of emotion. Once more, he realized it wasn't kissing her he needed, but her closeness, warmth and understanding. "I really want you to think about this, Katie."

Her lipstick was gone, her lips were glazed with the patina left by his mouth. "About...?"

"About the fact that I haven't stopped wanting you since the night we were first together," he whispered against her lips. "The night when..." His heart suddenly hammering, he curled his hand over her belly with fierce possessiveness. "The night when we made this baby, Katie."

He could barely hear her words; they were as soft as the dark, liquid night. "Let's just take this slow, Ford."

His eyes were like lasers on hers, telling her that whenever she wanted him, he'd be waiting. Life was so precious. Fleeting. Lincoln's death proved that, didn't it? His fingers flexing, the sage knit of her dress teasing his skin, Ford felt emotion double within him. Was she right? Could the new life she carried help mend the rift with his parents? Before his lips found hers again, he whispered, "Take it slow? Here's slow, Katie." And then he kissed her—very slow and very deep.

DAVID CARRINGTON stared into the starlit night, gazing from the window of his son's room across the expansive back lawn toward the stables. When a soft knock sounded against the door frame, he turned, raising a bushy gray eyebrow. "Are you done for the night, Yvonne?"

"Finally." Moving toward him, Yvonne slipped slender feet from her high-heeled shoes, stepping away from them as she pulled pins from her hair, letting the piled, coiled braids fall down her back. "The caterers left an hour ago, and the parking attendants are gone. I've been looking for you everywhere so we could talk."

David managed a smile as her arms circled his waist, and he took in their reflection in the mirror, as well as that of the room behind them—the antique dressers, an old oak bedstead where he'd tossed his tuxedo jacket on a plaid duvet. "I got on the phone," David said, "and called Johnny Newman."

"The lawyer?"

"I figured Ford's using him. And he is. Johnny says now that we know about the marriage, he'll courier the legal papers over tomorrow. The woman was pregnant before he married her, and she hired a tough attorney and got an iron-clad prenup. Johnny's worried about Ford. He says it's as if she was already planning a divorce."

Yvonne bit her lip. "Let's not jump to conclusions. Maybe Ford's finally found someone who..." She paused, and pain filled her eyes. "Someone who can love him in the way he needs, David. I know his marriage and the baby put us in a bind, but..."

A bind wasn't even the word for their position. Thrusting a hand through his steely hair, David continued staring at his reflection. Ever since the announcement in the ballroom, he'd felt as old as he looked. How long had it been since he and his son had exchanged pleasant words? he wondered, staring at the stables in the distance. "Ford knows the foundation's in trouble."

"He never involves himself with it, though, so he probably doesn't know the extent of the difficulties."

David shook his head. "Sure he does, Yvonne, but there's no use talking to him, and now he's married a woman who's obviously got her eyes on his wallet."

"You don't know that. Maybe she's simply trying to protect herself and the baby with the prenup."

Yvonne's voice caught. "She's pregnant, David. This is our grandchild…our first."

No one knew more than David how much Yvonne loved babies and children. "But if Ford takes the funds for the baby from the foundation…"

"They have the right to do so," Yvonne reminded him, her eyes darkening with what promised to become anger.

"Taking so much money right now would ruin the foundation," he argued. Tonight, he'd said the annual award allocations were delayed because competition was stiff. In reality, the foundation was cash poor. He and Yvonne and Gil were busy, freeing other investments so that the awards could be made later, and Gil was trying to convince his family to shift funds from the Gilcrest Endowment. Ten million dollars was more than the total of Carrington Foundation investments right now, so the loss would break them.

"Can we ask Ford to delay taking the money?" Yvonne suggested. "We could have Gil restructure the trust, so that it's no longer available at the baby's birth, but later. Say, on his or her eighteenth birthday. It's reasonable, and it would give us years to put the foundation on firm financial footing."

"Ford would never go for it," David said. "You saw him tonight. He came in, didn't even find me to say hello. Damn it, he'd like nothing more than to see the foundation ruined. Look at the way he let his new wife humiliate us tonight. Don't you see, Yvonne? He enjoys hurting us." David shook his head. He hadn't felt this badly since the day, years ago, when he'd broken down and confessed his one love affair, something Yvonne had found it in her heart to forgive. Not even his retirement from performing surgery at Texas General had made him this miserable. "For a long time now, Ford has ceased being a son," David continued. "He wants no part of us. And I won't let him ruin the foundation. My father started it, and it's been my life's work."

Yvonne watched him cautiously. "What are you going to do?"

David's jaw hardened. "Tell Ford the truth."

Yvonne inhaled sharply. "Oh, David, we can't! I won't let you!"

"After what he and his wife put us through tonight, it's time we call it quits." Yvonne might not be entirely supportive of his way of handling the situation, but he wasn't going to let Ford destroy him. "The truth," David repeated. "Who knows, Yvonne? Maybe he'll even feel freed by it."

Tears shimmered in Yvonne's eyes, and an expression of regret that went right to David's heart. "On this one, don't expect me to back you up."

His eyes panned the room. "Then don't," he returned stoically, adding in a soft mutter, "believe it or not, Yvonne, I *do* miss the boy."

Ford would have been amazed to know that the son's room in which his father was standing was his, not Lincoln's, and that the boy his father missed was him.


"WHY DO YOU THINK they asked us to come?" Katie whispered the next morning as they entered his father's study.

Ford frowned. "No idea." There was more to it than simply wanting to meet Katie, otherwise Gil Gilcrest wouldn't be present. The tall, angular man was standing before a towering window, his eyes sweeping the high ceilings, bookshelves and heavy furniture.

"Hello," Ford murmured as he and Katie seated themselves on a velvet settee. Reaching, he threaded his fingers through hers, and when she blushed Ford wondered if she was thinking of the closeness they'd shared in the car last night. As the others said hello, she shot him a quick smile of encouragement.

Ford smiled back, his gaze softening. Even though Katie was wearing jeans and a simple blouse, the calm way she folded her raincoat in her lap made her look more composed than any Carrington present. Glancing away, Ford took in his parents, who were seated on a settee opposite. Behind them, tall windows overlooked the front lawn and centuries-old trees with trunks so thick a man could hide behind them. *Lincoln's Landing,* Ford thought. It was easy to imagine a lot of grown men hiding here. Or getting lost.

Through the windows, the vast sky was cerulean, but despite the beautiful day, Ford had a sneaking suspicion the upcoming exchange would be ugly.

Gil said, "Thank you for coming."

Just watching the man, who, like his daughter, was regally tall and thin, unnerved Ford. "When you phoned this morning, Katie and I were happy to oblige," Ford offered, flexing his fingers reassuringly in hers. He'd intended to call and smooth things over, anyway. Now, he didn't care what his family did to him, he just didn't want anyone hurting Katie. Probably he shouldn't have brought her with him this morning. Last night, talking to her in the car had deepened his feelings, and while he'd left things at that second kiss, savoring the emotion behind it, it made him realize she deserved better. Funny, he thought. He, who seemed to have everything, was embarrassed by his family.

Gil looked as if he were searching for the right words. "Before I start, I hope you'll come to understand that we've no real choice but to…"

Ford glanced at Katie, glad to see she was holding her own. She'd been intimidated last night, but deep down, she was so sure of her own worth that she could have been a born Carrington. Cecil Nelson was right. She was a spitfire. "To?" Ford prompted.

"We don't want this to be difficult," David said, hedging.

Ford raised an eyebrow. "This?" When no one had the guts to continue, Ford said, "My guess is that you're going to give Katie and me trouble about her becoming a Carrington, or some such. Is that it?"

"Unfortunately," Gil continued, "it's a bit more problematical. You have every right to marry whomever you choose."

*No congratulations. No, we wish you well,* Ford thought, aware that somewhere deep inside him he harbored a vision of how things were supposed to be…a vision so clear that it pained him to look at it: there should be handshakes, gifts and a showering of good wishes. Katie should get hugs, kisses, and Yvonne should murmur that she'd always wanted a daughter.

*Yeah, right.* The closest thing to support his mother could muster for her son was to rise from his father's side. At the unusual display of disloyalty, Ford's senses went on alert, and he wondered if his father was going to contest the baby's right to the trust fund. Only his father would stoop so low. But how? Ford and Katie's rights were airtight. "Are you going to contest my grandfather's will?" Ford guessed, addressing Gil. "Are you trying to deny our baby's right to the trust fund?"

"Not the baby's right," Gil said. "Yours."

Ford's lips parted in bemused surprise. "You've outdone yourselves," he muttered. He was a Carrington born and bred. "On what grounds?"

Tears filled Yvonne's eyes. When no one spoke, she whispered, "Ford, I've asked them not to tell you this—"

"Yvonne," his father interjected in warning, the sound of his voice making Ford bristle.

"You were adopted, Ford," Yvonne said.

"So, legally, the trust isn't the baby's," added Gil, glancing away, his face hardening as if he were fighting down his more humane instincts. "Because of how the will's worded, the fund goes only to a blood Carrington." Gil heaved a sigh. "Damn it, I'm sorry, Ford, but the reality is that Lincoln was the last of the line."

Vaguely, Ford was aware of Gil's lifting papers from a file folder and offering proof. Ford's birth father was unknown, his mother dead. As Gil droned on, Ford was vaguely aware that Yvonne was brushing tears from her cheeks. The man he'd always thought of as his father was staring stoically straight ahead. Inside, Ford was reeling. Blood rushed in his ears, so loud it was drowning out the words. The whole world seemed to shift on its axis and spin in a new direction. Katie's free hand slid over his, feeling mildly damp and warm.

Yvonne said, "We tried to have a child for years, Ford, but we gave up...."

"Didn't give up," Ford managed to say, his tone terse, his heart pounding. "You got me." Bitterness curled inside him. "Bought me the way you do everything else, I guess."

Yvonne gasped. "Don't say such a thing, Ford. I was so happy with you that I wanted another baby. Seven years later, changes in medicine convinced your father and me to try...."

Ford couldn't even look at her. What the hell was happening here? How could someone else be his mother? "And that's when you had Lincoln?"

She nodded. "Yes. Yes, Ford."

His voice was low. "My grandfather didn't know."

"I spent the time I would have been pregnant with you abroad," she admitted. "We...your father and I didn't want anyone to know. At least not when you were little. We wanted to insure you had the respect of this family's name. We wanted to raise you as our own. Completely ours..."

So, Lincoln had been their only natural born son. Katie's fingers squeezed his, and right then, Ford felt as if she was the only thing anchoring him to the world. Somehow, he squeezed back as her other hand, so soft and cool, glided back and forth over his. *Oh, God, Katie. No wonder they hated me after the accident, especially Dad. Lincoln was his only son. I wasn't.* "My grandfather would never do this to me," he said, fighting the emotions and thinking of the old man who'd died when he was seventeen. *He loved me*.

"No," Yvonne murmured. "We never told him. David's father set such a great store by blood relations, and he finally had a child to carry on the family name."

Stunned, Ford could only stare at Yvonne and David Carrington, the people he'd called his parents for so many years. Now he felt as if he'd never seen them before. Yvonne's hair was golden, just like Lincoln's. She had dark eyes, but a color unlike Ford's. He resembled neither of them, now that he really looked. How had he not noticed before? Why hadn't people remarked on it? His eyes stung, feeling gritty.

"He wasn't the only one obsessed with genealogy and family trees," Ford muttered. "I imagine it was difficult for you to accept another woman's child as your own, too. Given you're the charter member of the Texas Genealogical Society."

His mother looked startled. "Genealogy's a hobby, Ford."

Holding on to Katie's hand, he stood up, feeling her quiet strength as she rose beside him. He'd never needed anybody as he needed her at this moment. "I've felt guilty over the years," he found himself saying, his voice strained with thwarted love, rejection and suppressed fury. "I blamed myself for Lincoln's death and tried to make up for your grief. But this? Would you have told me if your precious foundation hadn't been threatened?"

"Two projects begun last year can't be finished now," David said, his voice tight. "One is the Carrington Medical Training Center, a multimillion-dollar project downtown, and the other is the Carrington Clinic. Last night, I couldn't make allocations for this year's projects. If we didn't tell you, if you took that money, the foundation would close.''

*If they'd only said so.* ''But it never occurred to you to ask for my help, did it? Or to use my investment knowledge to raise the cash you need? No, instead, you use the occasion of my marriage and coming child to drop this bombshell.'' He swallowed hard before forging on. ''To make clear that Lincoln was your real son. More important than me. But the truth is, the foundation was your baby, wasn't it? You didn't need me. If Lincoln had lived, the truth is you wouldn't have needed him, either. You sure as hell don't want a grandbaby.''

Yvonne uttered a sharp cry, but Ford steeled himself against her. She might have feelings for him, she might even love him, but she'd always been the woman behind the man, and Ford's father was as cold as ice. ''Ford, don't leave,'' she begged. ''Say something....''

''All right. I'll say something. You two deserve each other,'' said Ford. ''You want me to stick around and fight with him, the way I always do, but not this time, Mother. Consider our relations severed. Katie and I are leaving. And this time, we won't be coming back.''

## CHAPTER SIX

How could Yvonne and David Carrington use their grandchild's conception to deliver such startling news to their son? Katie wondered, still feeling shocked. Withdrawing her hands from the pockets of a forest-green sweat suit, she glanced around Ford's guest room, pulling a battered Samsonite suitcase onto the canopied bed and placing a folded stack of faded jeans inside. "Unbelievable," she murmured, sadness and surprise mixing with anger.

Oh, there were hurt feelings all around, Katie had seen that right off. Ford had looked murderous, and David Carrington had been suited up for battle, wearing his starched shirt, jacket and arrow-straight tie like jousting armor, his thick silver hair so neatly plastered to his head that it looked like a warrior's helmet. "Dressed," Katie murmured, "for the all-important task of breaking Ford's heart, I suppose." Despite his quivering chin, David had been hell bent on communicating that he didn't need anybody, least of all Ford. "As high and mighty as David Carrington looks, he's driven by ordinary, average, everyday emotions," Katie whispered. "Riddled with vulnerabilities." So was Yvonne, who seemed torn between the two men. If David hadn't been present, Katie was sure she would have acknowledged their coming grandchild.

Katie glanced around the room again, her heart aching as she took in the high, firm bed she wouldn't be sleeping in tonight. Its white spread was turned back, and gold tassels on the embroidered pillows coiled on red satin sheets.

*I don't want to leave Ford.*

No, she wanted to be in that bed with him, holding him in her arms. He'd said he wanted to be alone, though, and now, when Katie thought of the dark, haunted cast of his eyes on the silent drive from his folks', she knew he was shutting her out. The lack of love he'd been shown made her chest swell with feeling, just as surely as it seemed to be making him unreachable. Walls as high and stony as those circling the Carrington estate had risen around him since their return. Should she continue packing? Or should she wait for Ford to mention her leaving, since there was no longer any real reason for him to be married to her? No doubt, given these new circumstances, he'd want an annulment.

"Of course he will," she whispered. Ford wanted to get to know her, and he wanted her sexually, but that didn't make for a real marriage. If she didn't pack, wouldn't it be presumptuous? Her heart lurched. Right now, the last thing he needed was extra pressure. Surely, once she was resettled in her apartment, Ford would visit. The feelings they'd begun to explore, while not enough to make a marriage, were too important to forget. She hoped he'd give them a chance to grow. He definitely wanted to be part of the pregnancy. Used to feeling unloved, he was trying to hide his emotions, but he was so excited about being a dad.

Sighing, Katie took a fistful of panties from a drawer, dropped them into the suitcase, then forced herself to head for the closet. The rich, lush green carpet felt so soft that she could have been running barefoot on the farm, feeling wet earth oozing between her toes after a rainfall. "It feels like pure money," she murmured. "And it's hard to enjoy it at the moment." She'd give anything necessary—ten million dollars or a dime, she didn't care—not to have Ford look so hurt.

As she slipped her good sage dress from a hanger, images of the times she'd worn it flashed through her mind—her and Ford's wedding, their kisses in the car last night. Inhaling a quick breath, she thought of how he'd toyed with the neckline, dipping a finger beneath it before he left her at the bedroom door. By the time she'd awakened this morning, his parents had summoned them, and so, without so much as another kiss, they'd rushed out the door.

"Wonder what his folks thought of this morning's newspaper?" she muttered, shaking her head. The fellow with whom she'd traded the flute of apple juice had turned out to be a reporter. Somehow, he'd discovered Katie's nickname, so the society page headline read Dangling Carrot?

Katie "Carrot Top" Carrington, the man claimed, was a breath of fresh air, who would breathe new life into the Carrington Foundation. So many people from Maitland Maternity had called after reading the article that Katie had unplugged the phone, not wanting it to disturb Ford. She had talked to Jem and Gary. But what would she and Ford tell people at the hospital tomorrow?

Still unsure about whether she should be packing, Katie stilled her hand on the suitcase. Her brothers had been sworn to secrecy until their papa's return from Dallas, but knowing them, they'd blab the news at the first opportunity. Earlier this morning, Katie had thought that might be just as well. By the time she told her papa, maybe Jem and Gary would have softened him up. Now, if there would soon be no marriage, Katie didn't even want to imagine Jack Topper's reaction to her out-of-wedlock pregnancy.

*But maybe Ford feels as you do,* a voice niggled. *Maybe whatever's happening between you is more important than trying to set up the trust for the baby.*

Glancing toward the door, she wondered how Ford was doing. As far as she knew, he was still outside, sitting in a patio chair, huddled in a hooded sweatshirt jacket. She'd stood in the window earlier, for nearly an hour, watching him and wanting to go to him. He looked so heartbreakingly lonely, his hands thrust deeply into his pockets, forlorn tufts of breath clouding the air, his face hard and implacable. He'd looked every inch the driven, uncompromising surgeon whose sharp gaze stared down death for hour on end. He was a man to be reckoned with, Katie had thought, staring at him from the bedroom window, a man to be admired, but one who might ultimately be more feared than loved.

And yet she cared for him so much.

So, should she stay, hoping he wouldn't ask her to leave? "Oh, Katie, where's your pride?" she murmured. Impulsively, she lifted the sage dress from the suitcase and pressed it to her face. She was still inhaling the lingering male scent of Ford's cologne when the partially cracked bedroom door swung open the rest of the way.

She glanced up. "Ford?"

"Katie."

"When did you come in?" She hadn't heard him.

"Just a few minutes ago."

He'd changed clothes, and maybe because he was shirtless and barefoot, the first thing she noticed when he leaned in the doorway wasn't his face, but the thick black hair tunneling down his chest, swirling around his navel and vanishing beneath his waistband. When he shoved his hands deep into the pockets of his faded jeans, the movement called attention to his thick, ropelike veins and corded forearms. Lovingly worn denim cupped the soft protrusion of his maleness. Only when he used a powerful shoulder to push himself from the door frame did she realize she was staring at him like an idiot, with her dress pressed to her nose. She felt as if she'd been caught sniffing Ford's scent like a female dog in heat. Blushing, she uttered a quick, "How are you feeling now?" and finished folding the dress, placing it in the suitcase.

He didn't answer. His eyes were panning the room, taking in a sock that dangled from a drawer, then the open closet. With a rush of pity, she acknowledged he was trying to mask the raw hurt he'd experienced. "Going somewhere?" he asked.

The tone took her aback. "Uh...home." Of course she was. Or was she? Her heart thudded dully. Did he feel as she did? Did he want her to stay? "When we got back from your folks', you said you wanted to be alone, and since we both have to work tomorrow, I thought…''

''I thought you said you wanted to get to know me better, Katie.'' His movements were smooth but calculating as he strode into the room, glancing inside her suitcase with deceptive casualness.

Her heart squeezed tight. ''I do, Ford. I've wanted to ever since we first met.''

''Yeah, right. So you said. But don't let me detain you.''

He sounded every bit as cold as his folks, reminding her that he'd come from a world she didn't fully understand…a world where caring and affection didn't necessarily come in tandem. ''Ford…''

As she murmured his name, he edged so close that she could feel the heat emanating from all that very bare male skin. His scent was palpable, too, just as it had been on the dress she'd worn last night—sharp, but subtle, earthy but clean, arousing and male. Her eyes strayed once more to the curling black hairs swirling toward his low-slung waistband, and the pull of her heart was so strong she nearly stepped forward. Oh, yes, she wanted to touch him. She wanted to stroke his bare waist, and lower still. She wanted to wrap her arms tightly around him, soothing his demons. She could barely find her voice. ''Do you want me to stay, Ford?''

He eyed her, looking as if he'd come here with every intention of unloading some of his anger—or worse, as if he wanted to construe her leaving as something his folks had caused, so he could further build a case in his mind against them. ''Ford,'' she continued carefully, ''you asked me to marry you because of the trust, and I want to get to know you better, but now, given what we've found out…''

He scrutinized the suitcase's contents, casually lifting a handful of her panties, then a belt. His jaw hardened, and suddenly he looked dark, angry and disconcertingly sensual. His gaze, when he raised it from the suitcase, drifted curiously up her sweat suit. Every blessed, pleasurable thing the man had ever done to her came racing back, the touch of his eyes alone eliciting a response as surely as if he'd touched her. His body stiffened when he noticed her reaction, and Katie suddenly felt as if she'd explode. How could so much male-female tension exist between two people? The room was as quiet as a tomb. Her throat felt scratchy and raw. "Do you want me to stay, Ford?" she repeated.

He was staring at her as if she'd committed some cardinal sin. "The question is whether or not you really want to leave, isn't it, Katie?"

She hesitated. She'd cared for him for years, but telling him how much wasn't a risk she was ready to take. She didn't want to admit to feelings he didn't share.

"I only said I wanted to be alone for a while, Katie," he added.

*Not forever.* "I wasn't trying to hurt you."

Either her words touched some deep wound, or he was reacting to the pity she couldn't keep from her eyes, because when he spoke, his words were too measured. "Believe me, you're not."

He said it as if she weren't any more important than a speck on the wall. "Don't do this," she murmured. "Don't pretend nothing touches you."

"Maybe nothing can."

"Our baby has." She watched his throat work as he swallowed, and she thrust a hand deeply into the pocket of her sweatpants, wedging a thigh against the bed and using the mattress for support. "I can't imagine what you're going through," she added.

He shrugged, glanced away. "They're not even my parents, Katie."

"Sure they are."

"Not anymore."

She couldn't imagine finding out Jack Topper wasn't her biological father. Would shared blood have stemmed the tide of the Carringtons' power struggle, which she'd witnessed today? she wondered. Cupping a hand to her belly, she made a sudden, silent vow to never wrong her child. *Mine and Ford's.* The reminder of their deeper connection made her voice even gentler. "They'll always be your folks."

Fury touched his eyes as they bored into hers. "For God's sake, I've been on my own a long time. I'm a grown man, Katie."

No denying that, she thought, suppressing a shiver as her eyes trailed over him. But then, age never stopped anybody from needing love. "I wish I knew one word or phrase that would make things all right."

"Don't try to play nice."

"I'm not playing," she assured him, knowing he came from a place where people did play sometimes, hiding their genuine feelings. "I *am* nice."

"Really?" His voice lowered, growing so thick with emotion that Katie heard the syrupy Texas drawl he thought he'd lost years ago. "Seems to me you're here when it suits you. Gone when it doesn't. Suddenly, there's no paycheck in this for you and the baby…and *poof.* It's back to the farm for Katie Topper.''

"Katie Carrington," she corrected, trying not to react, her knowledge of his pain allowing her to tamp down her temper. "And I was headed for my apartment, not the farm.''

"What about your father? Won't he be angry if you're not living with your husband?"

"I'm worried about what he'll say," she admitted.

"What he'll say?" Ford's lips set in a grim line. He growled, "It'd be nice if you cared about *me* a little.''

"Cared about you?" she echoed. "You know I do. I'm the most compassionate woman you'll ever meet, too, but I'm also beginning to think you came in here looking for a fight.''

"You *are* running the second you see I've got nothing to offer.''

Nothing to offer? It must have taken such a lack of love to convince Ford of that. Distractedly, she lifted some socks from the bed and tossed them into the suitcase, wishing she didn't feel so confused. One second, she was Ford's most supportive advocate, the next, she was furious. Not just at him, but at his family for giving him a mind-set that left him feeling so unlovable.

"I thought you went to Houston to learn about the human heart," he told her. "Maybe you didn't learn as much as you thought you did.''

Yes, he was definitely looking for an argument. "I'm telling you, Ford. You'd better be careful.''

"Careful?"

"Yeah. Or I'll think you're suggesting I'm a working-class climber," she said with a toss of her head. "Somebody who's just out for your money." Stepping past him, feeling strangely on the verge of tears, she rapidly packed some T-shirts. Wishing his damnable gaze wasn't following her, she felt her self-consciousness increase under the intense perusal, until her movements turned jerky and unnatural. Unable to take the tension, she turned from the suitcase, placing her hands on her hips. "Do you know what drives me crazy about you?"

Damn if he didn't look as if he was starting to love every minute of this. "What? Go ahead. Get it out of your system."

She released a throaty, derisive chuckle, as if to say she was above all this. "You think *I'm* leaving because you have nothing to offer? *You're* the one who thinks people care about status and money, Ford. What about your surgical talent? Or your business acumen, or your ability to hold up under pressure, or your sense of humor and perseverance—" Realizing she was merely complimenting him, Katie broke off. As she stepped away again, mostly to evade the searing heat of his eyes, she felt his fingers wrap around her upper arm.

"Look at me, Katie."

Those strong fingers closed more tightly—not unpleasantly, she hated to admit—around her arm until she was flush against him, her breasts pressing against his hard bare chest. She shivered. Warm prickles shimmered down her spine, knotting at the small of her back when she felt unwanted heat seeping through his jeans to her pelvis.

He drew in an audible breath, then silkily, huskily, murmured, "Just look at me."

Her throat tightened. Either that, or a lump lodged there unexpectedly. "I don't have much choice, do I, Ford?"

"Fine." His voice dropped a notch, sounding strangely unsteady. "Feel free to pack."

Silently, she damned him for touching her pride, especially since she'd wanted to show him every kindness right now. "Feel free?" she couldn't help but murmur, her eyes fixing on his. "Isn't that a little imperious, Ford? I'm not a slave." *I'm your wife. Please, Ford, tell me to stay. Tell me you want to try to make this last.*

His dark eyes narrowed, and despite her confusion, she couldn't help but notice the wonderful things that did to his face—sharpening his high, strong cheekbones, making the corners of his eyes crinkle. He whispered, "Really, Katie. Just pack."

Tears sprang to her eyes. "If you'd let me go," she forced herself to say, "I would."

The swift, unexpected hoarseness that claimed his voice took her by surprise. "Damn it, Katie. Forget I said that. Don't go. I don't know what I'm saying right now. I'm just mad."

As tactile as a touch, she could feel the words— their weight and substance. Curling inside her, they burrowed deep, to her very core, but she still couldn't quite believe she'd heard them. "You want me to stay?" Her voice was scarcely audible. "To live with you?"

He sounded tentative. "At least until the baby's born—"

*But after that? What then?* "There's a future after the baby," she had to tell him. "Don't you see, Ford? The longer I stay now, the harder it will be later."

Glancing away, he released a short, frustrated breath as if he found it difficult to say the words. "I know. But I don't know what to say. I can't promise a future right now, Katie. No more than you can promise you'd want one with me. But this is our chance to see. This is my baby, too, just like it's yours." A large, wind-tanned hand settled boldly on her waist; the other smoothed gently over her belly. "Mine," he repeated, his voice touching the word like a hot brand. "I think about us having this child all the time. I can't tell you what it means to me. I feel like..." Briefly, he glanced away before his eyes returned to hers. "Like it's my chance to have my own family. Maybe I can get it right this time. I'm going through this pregnancy with you, Katie. I want you here."

The words ripped at her heart, and her hands crept to his chest. "I think about the baby, too." Swallowing hard, she lifted her gaze honestly to his. "I wanted to stay, Ford. I didn't want to pack, but I didn't want to pressure you." *Or to risk my heart.* Too many times, she'd imagined deepening their physical relationship, moving into his bedroom, having long, softly murmured conversations about their future. If she gave any more of herself and things didn't work out, she was so afraid she couldn't survive the hurt. The hand on her belly was sending such sharp sensations through her body that her knees weakened. Her heart stretched to breaking.

"Then stay," he said. "And I'll take my parents

to court," he added vengefully, lifting a hand and running his palm over his head, slicking back his thick, lush hair. "My grandfather set up this trust. If he'd known the truth, he'd never have worded it as he did. He meant to give our baby everything, Katie, just as he meant for me to take over the foundation someday."

Wondering at Ford's motivations, she said, "Would you?"

"Would I what?"

"Have taken over the foundation?"

"Yeah. Not that it matters now. My father's made too much of an issue over it." Ford sighed wearily. "They could have used my business sense. But they didn't. And now I'm going to fight them." His voice steadied with conviction. "We've got a case. If you stay, we can get our settlement."

She didn't know whether to laugh or cry. Ford didn't really care about the money, that had been clear on the drive to see his parents, but he felt they didn't love him, and he wanted to hurt them because of it. Deep down, he wanted strong relationships with them. He wanted to help them run the foundation. "A settlement," she repeated, hoping he could hear how ludicrous it sounded. "Is that why you want me to stay?"

His eyes fixed on hers. "Partly."

She was out of her league, she realized, involved in a wealthy family's power struggle with her own heart at risk. "You care more about the foundation than you'll admit," she pointed out carefully. "You care about me, too. But you also want to hurt your father. I don't want you using me to do it."

"I'm not using you, Katie."

There was no use protesting, but she recalled his pleasure at the Carrington Foundation party when she'd caused such a stir. If she stayed, it would strengthen his case if he contested the will.

"My father deserves whatever he gets, Katie," he added.

"No," she corrected. "He needs a lesson in loving." Given that, she was hard-pressed not to forgive Ford's attitude. David Carrington had dealt his son an unforgivable blow today. But was Ford really angry enough to take him to court? And did he need her right now simply because he felt so abandoned by his family? Suddenly, she wished her traitorous mouth would form the shortest, most complete sentence in the English language—no. She really shouldn't stay here under these circumstances. Instead, she said, "I'll stay under one condition."

"Condition?"

"I don't want you taking your dad to court."

Even as a silken finger trailed down her cheek, Ford's jaw set with determination. "It's the right thing to do, Katie."

"No, it's not," she returned, her voice catching. "Think of our baby."

"I am," said Ford.

"No, you're not. He or she is going to need a daddy whose mind is preoccupied with love, not vengeance."

"Stay," Ford repeated. "And I'll think about it."

HOURS LATER, Ford found himself in Katie's doorway once more. "Get enough to eat for dinner, Carrot

Top?'' Leaning against the door frame, he glanced into the room she'd tidied, and as his gaze settled on the empty Samsonite propped against the wall, he felt a rush of relief.

She was smiling. "Burned burgers. My favorite."

"That's why you ate three?"

"Two."

"Three."

She chuckled, and his smile surprised him. Today had been one of the worst of his life. For years, he realized, he'd moved in a superficial world he despised. Now, suddenly, he was someplace else: in a world where his parents weren't really his own... where he was about to be a father...where a warm, emotional woman was in his life.

Everything had changed.

Sitting outside, he'd tried to center himself as he often did before performing difficult surgeries. Had his adoptive parents felt any real love for him? he'd wondered. Did they really blame him for Lincoln's death? Looking at Katie, he felt another rush of anger mesh with wistful longing. He half suspected that Katie Topper Carrington was too kind a person to understand how he felt. Damn right he was taking his family to court. He just wouldn't tell Katie about it.

"You'll get through all this," she encouraged him.

"Enough nights like tonight, and maybe I will." Despite the chilly air, they'd gone outside and fired up the gas grill. While Katie watched from a lawn chair, cuddled in a plaid camp blanket, he'd cooked. He added, "Thanks for putting up with me earlier."

Her understanding eyes said it all. "I can't imagine..."

*What I'm going through.* "I can't, either."

During dinner, the sheer warmth of her presence had soothed him. Every time he looked at Katie, the cold dark night seemed to turn into a warm spring day. Right now, they could be sitting outside, wiggling their bare toes in tall grass, breathing the scent of spring flowers. But it was winter. And they were inside. And Katie was still living here. *Thank God.* Her heavily lidded eyes were sexy, her mouth pouty. She said, "I think you'll be just fine, Ford. Want to know why?"

She was gazing at him through her lashes, and he could see just enough of her eyes to register her emotions. "Why?"

"Because of the way you work in the OR. You're determined to pull through, no matter what. You're like me, Ford. We never let life get us down."

Maybe. But earlier today, a chasm had opened inside him like a black hole, threatening to engulf him. "We don't, huh?" He thought of his brother, the brother who had never been his flesh and blood, then he thought of how Katie had lost her mother when she was young, something she'd talked about during dinner. "I guess I am a survivor, Katie."

"Me, too. It's so long ago now that my mother died. But it's still always there, that sense of loss."

Offering a sad smile, he watched her, listening to the old house that had belonged to his grandfather. The last creaks and groans had diminished, the lights were dimmed, the doors and windows locked.

"It's settling down for the night," she whispered, seemingly reading his mind.

"It's a house meant for a family," he returned,

feeling a sudden pang and not caring if what he'd said was too revealing. "I want a family. Maybe we've got more in common than we ever realized, Katie."

"I never said we didn't." She swallowed hard. "And you've got a family, Ford. You're just fighting with them right now."

He molded a hand down the warm half-moon of her hip; the other he curled around her neck. Releasing a low, shuddering sigh, he nodded down the hallway toward his room. "Can you come to bed with me tonight, Katie?"

He could tell she wanted to, but she only smiled, a slow, apologetic smile as if to say she needed to process all that was happening to them. "Not tonight."

*Not yet, Ford.*

When? His lungs emptied as her hand slid around his waist, the inconsequential touch making his heart hammer. The scent of her hair tortured him as he nuzzled a cheek to her temple, and his voice came out sounding as rough as sandpaper. "If you won't come to my bed tonight, Katie…will you at least kiss me?"

Her voice was a soft rasp. "Yeah. I'll lighten you up, too."

He stroked her neck. "Lighten me up?"

She nodded, looking pleased with herself. "I'll take you out to the farm. Jem and Gary will straighten you out."

At the thought of roughhousing at the Toppers' five-acre spread—riding over the rolling hills and sharing raucous yells and chores with Katie's brothers—Ford's relief deepened. "What?" he murmured. "Are you going to show me what family's all about?"

She looked almost mischievous. "Yeah."

A slow smile lifted his lips. "Thanks."

A dreamy tone took the threat from her words. "You won't be thanking me when I put you to work."

His smile broadened. "Going to take it out of my hide?"

"You won't know what hit you."

His heart suddenly aching, he whispered, "Already, I don't, Katie." Moments from now, he'd be lying in the dark, painfully aware of her presence, fantasizing about her perfect legs and silken curves, about firm breasts that needed suckling. His smile vanished as emotion filled him. Slowly, he brushed a thumb across her lower lip, the touch lingering at the corners. "No, Katie," he sighed. "I really don't know what's hit me." He pressed his lips to hers then, and her mouth yielded with excruciating gentleness. Feeling strangely bereft when he drew away, he whispered, "Good night then, Katie."

Her wide green eyes were fixed on his, and the soft, shuddering whisper of her breath made him think she might change her mind and come to bed with him.

But she only whispered, "Good night."

STANDING in the bed of Jem's red pickup, Katie pushed away her deeper thoughts and waved jauntily at Ford and her brothers. "Ride 'em, cowboys!" she shouted.

Turning in the saddle, Ford lifted his hat. Waving

once more, she lowered the tailgate, then unfolded lawn chairs, arranging them in the truck bed. Once she was done, she stared toward the makeshift team-penning arena. For years, the Toppers, like many other families, had come here on Friday nights to play cowboy. Two spotlights illuminated the riding ring. At one end, twenty head of cattle huddled; at the opposite end a smaller, interior pen had been fenced off. The cattle's ears were tagged with numbered yellow markers, and soon the announcer would call out the numbers. The three riders in the ring would attempt to pen those cows.

Jem trotted closer to the fence. Lifting his pride and joy—a Stetson Katie had gotten him a year ago for Christmas—the nineteen-year-old held it against a T-shirt printed with the logo of an Austin country music station. Tweaking the handlebar mustache he'd recently grown, he called out, "Why aren't you riding, sis?"

Her brothers knew she'd eloped with Ford, but not about the pregnancy. "Because I want to see you guys lose."

Jem smirked. "Okay, hotshot. You just watch and see if we don't win without you this time."

She swatted her backside. "Kiss my round Irish behind," she taunted, then she sighed happily. Shivering against the cold, she draped a green camp blanket around her shoulders and double-checked a cooler that she and Ford had filled with everything from her homemade pimento cheese to peanut butter and jelly sandwiches.

The night was dark and cold, but no one cared. All around the truck, riders were walking down horses or queuing up for two-minute rides while kids played tag in an adjacent field, squealing with delight as they zigzagged around horse trailers.

"C'mon, Katie—" Jem trotted to the fence again. "We need you on this next ride. Gary says he'll sit it out. You're ten times better than he is."

"I knew you'd beg," she called. "I *am* the only one of you who has a chance of penning those cows."

"What ego!" her brother taunted, trotting away once more.

This event drew weekend cowboys, and unlike trained rodeo cattle, the field cows got upset when asked to do anything more complicated than chew grass. That meant it was rare, if ever, that riders actually penned them. It was one reason Katie loved spending her Friday nights here when she wasn't needed at the hospital. Competition at the event was kept to a minimum. Everybody came for simple, good old-fashioned fun.

"C'mon, Katie." In a put-on Texas drawl even thicker than his usual one, Jem crooned, "If you ride, we might pen one of those ornery critters."

"You just want that twenty-dollar winning purse," she accused.

"Katie—" Gary steadied himself by pressing his palomino's flanks while he retied the red ponytail he wore down his back. "You've got no family feeling."

"Not an ounce," she asserted, shooting a glance at Ford, who'd come closer. Staring down from Huge Luther, he winked. She smirked, feeling a rush of mild annoyance. She would have ridden, but having a doctor as the father of your baby had its disadvantages. So far, she and Ford agreed about everything from diet to vitamins, but all the way to the arena, they'd tangled like wildcats, with him forbidding her to ride because of her condition.

"Clumsy men fall off horses all the time!" she'd argued.

"They're not pregnant, Katie," he'd said.

"And they couldn't get pregnant if their lives depended on it," she'd agreed grumpily. His need to protect her was so sweet that she'd finally let him win. Trouble was, her brothers expected her to ride, and they couldn't understand why she wouldn't. Deeper emotion grew inside her; she wished riding was all she and Ford were arguing about. Yesterday, a lawyer named Johnny Newman called, and she'd discovered Ford had lied. He was planning to contest his grandfather's will, after all.

"Let me handle this my way," he'd said when she confronted him.

"I told you I'd only stay if you didn't take them to court," she'd returned, even though she couldn't quite bring herself to leave him. And yet how could she stand by, watching Ford's vengeful nature destroy the very thing he wanted most—a relationship with his family? How, with his own family issues unresolved, could Ford even contemplate starting a family with her? Why couldn't he understand that tangling with his folks in front of a judge's bench would alienate them forever? Not only would he lose his folks, but he'd jeopardize their unborn child's relations with them, as well.

She realized Jem was watching her and she managed a smile. "Sorry, but you'll have to win without me tonight, Jem."

"You know how Katie is," Ford joked, raising his voice. "She wants to stay in the back of the pickup, making me those pimento cheese sandwiches. Right, honey?"

Gary laughed so hard he choked.

"And just when I was beginning to think you were a smart guy, Ford," Jem teased. "Katie'll chew you up and spit you out before you even know what happened."

"None of your surgeon friends will be able to put you back together again," agreed Gary.

Ford was about to respond when the announcer's voice sounded over the loudspeaker. "Riders at the ready!"

As Jem, Gary and Ford trotted farther into the ring, Katie rose, excitement coursing through her. A bell was struck, and the three men took off at a gallop. Just before they reached the cows, the announcer called, "Number fours. You cowboys herd all the cattle tagged with the number four. That's three cows, boys, each tagged with the number four."

"Fours!" Katie shoved a hand in the back pocket of her jeans and rose on tiptoe. The cows tagged with the number four were all bony, ragtag Herefords. "Those cows wouldn't go into the pen if you shot 'em up with tranquilizer and hand-carried them! They'd faint from walking that far!"

As she heaved a sigh of frustration, she heard Ford yell, "Right there! Get him, Gary!" Gary rushed two head toward Ford, his ponytail flying, then Ford ran them down the length of the ring.

"All right!" she shouted as Ford shooed one into the pen.

He was good. She hated to admit it, but Ford could teach her a few things about horses. He might have secretly wanted to go into business once, and maybe medicine wasn't in his blood, but he would have made a fine cowboy. Animals could sense his lack of fear, and they responded to him.

"Or maybe not," she whispered, watching as the cow he'd penned escaped. Fortunately, a few seconds later, another walked inside.

"Time," a voice boomed over the loudspeaker. "Sorry, cowboys, but your two minutes are up!"

"Good try!" shouted Katie. "You penned one!"

"We penned them all," Ford shouted. "You must not have been watching. You missed it."

Losing didn't bother her brothers any more than it did Ford. Waving, they trotted past, heading for the horse trailers. Ford threw a long, lean leg over Huge Luther's sturdy back, swung down, tied the reins to the truck's trailer hitch and hopped into the truck bed.

"You'd better walk down my horse," Katie warned. "He needs to cool off."

"I will." Ford leaned down and flipped open the lid of the cooler.

"Let me guess. You need a beer first."

Ford cracked the tab of a soda and took a gulp. "No, I need to kiss a lady friend."

Katie glanced around. "See any ladies."

Twining his fingers through hers, Ford pulled her from the lawn chair, swiftly turned, took the chair for himself, then pulled her into his lap, wrapping the blanket around them both. She smiled at him, circling her arms around his neck, wishing she could bring up the legal case again, but not wanting to ruin the moment, especially since the cold night was so strangely delicious—making her nose and cheeks cold, making her want to seek Ford's warmth.

"You're warm," he murmured as if reading her mind.

"I can get warmer."

"Prove it."

"I might, one of these days."

"What about now?" Rustling his hands into her hair, he pulled her face down for a wet, thorough kiss. His cheek felt cold against hers, his tongue an explosion of heat inside her mouth. It flickered against hers with familiar intimacy, and when he drew back, she gazed down pensively.

"What are you thinking, Katie?"

*About where our relationship's heading.* "That it's good to see you smile." Katie had hoped Yvonne would talk to her husband, or call and attempt a reconciliation, but she hadn't. Never would, either, if Ford took them to court. Nevertheless, Ford looked happy right now, relaxed. Maybe spending time with Jem and Gary would help convince him to mend bridges with his family. She'd hate to see Ford unleash his focus, strength and hard-edged perseverance in court. Her throat tightening with emotion, she caught his hand, curling it against her belly, where the pregnancy was just starting to show. *Here's another reason to love, instead of seeking vengeance.* Resituating herself in his lap, she whispered, "Having fun?"

"Yeah. I like riding with your brothers, Katie." Ford snuggled the blanket around her shoulders, a shadow of emotion momentarily darkening his sparkling eyes. He seemed far away for a second, maybe back in the stables at Lincoln's Landing.

"I know you do." Could her brothers become like the brother Ford lost? Her eyes softening, she realized there was so much Ford didn't know about love, so many things she wanted to teach him. One was that it extended beyond a man and woman. Whatever was happening between them had to include her family and his. Taking a deep breath, she thought of her papa. He'd be back soon, before she and Ford resolved their issues. No doubt he'd expect to meet the Carringtons. Pushing aside the thoughts, she smiled. "Thought you were interested in kissing a lady friend, Ford."

Right before his lips claimed hers again, Ford grinned. "Absolutely, Carrot Top."

# CHAPTER SEVEN

"I'LL GET IT!" Katie called when a security bell rang, announcing a car was passing through the front gate, heading toward the house. "Bet it's Jem and Gary." Last night, she'd asked them over for dinner.

"Tell them they've got to help me put on the steaks," Ford returned from the den.

"They'll want to look at the horses first, but don't you dare let them talk you into taking your thoroughbreds to Friday night team penning. I mean it, Ford. Those horses are too good for that kind of riding."

"Snob. Who says Kentucky Derby stock can't team pen?"

On her way to the front door, Katie leaned around the archway leading into the den and smiled. Ford was sitting cross-legged in his favorite leather armchair, wearing jeans and a turtleneck as jet black as his hair. When he glanced up from the medical thriller he was reading, she said, "Are we eating in there, Ford?"

"Up to you. But I thought it might be nice. We could watch a video while we eat, now that I've discovered movies are your secret passion."

Her gaze shifted to the novel. She'd never have guessed his secret hankering to use his medical knowledge to write a thriller, or that their shared love

"I'm not exactly a Sphinx, standing guard," Katie assured her with sudden decision, lifting a hand and smoothing her hair as she opened the door wider and stepped back. "Please come in. I'm sure he'll be happy you've come."

"Happy?" From a scant foot away, Ford's low voice sounded dangerous. "Really? What on earth would make you say such a thing, Carrot Top?"

She whirled, wincing. How had he approached so quietly? And how could his mood turn surly so quickly? He was glaring at her as if she'd betrayed him, and while she couldn't exactly blame him, she hoped he'd make an effort with his mother. Instead, he lounged in the archway, his hands thrust deeply into jeans pockets, the pose deceptively relaxed, his gaze darkly detached. "It's your mother," Katie finally ventured, mustering a bright tone.

"I know who she is." His eyes flashed, settling on Katie. "So, did you know she was coming?"

Taken aback, Katie blinked. Did he really think she'd invite Yvonne without telling him? "No." She forced herself to reply politely, shooting Yvonne a quick smile. "It's a surprise."

Yvonne's fingers stilled on the shoulder strap, curling around it so tightly that her knuckles whitened. "I certainly didn't come to cause trouble."

"Really?" Ford's gaze shifted to Yvonne, and as it panned the plush foyer, red-carpeted stairs, and wide hallway, his voice lowered, sounding oddly lazy, almost lethal. "Maybe you've realized this house belonged to Grandfather Carrington, Mother? Maybe you've come to reclaim it?"

Despite her self-possessed posture, Yvonne seemed

shaky, as though she were fighting not to appear vulnerable. The hand that wasn't clutching the strap of her bag curled over the doorknob. "Don't make this difficult."

Ford's boredom was feigned, but that didn't make it any less cutting. "Me? You came here uninvited."

Yvonne lifted her chin a defensive notch that Katie suspected would only further anger Ford. Had she done the wrong thing? she wondered. Should she have asked Yvonne to leave? She'd been trying to mend fences, not weaken them.

"Please, Ford." Yvonne's voice was measured. "I'm your mother."

"Hardly. Wasn't that the whole point of our last meeting?"

Yvonne straightened her shoulders, rapidly blinking her eyes as if fighting tears. "Your father and I would have told you the truth about your adoption, but the books we consulted said it was best to tell a child after puberty. And then...and then..."

"Lincoln died." Ford nodded curtly, as if to say this was exactly what he expected. "After that, you didn't want much to do with me, isn't that right? You blamed me, didn't you?"

Katie's heart squeezed. For a second, there seemed to be a weight inside her, pulling her down. Why couldn't Ford understand that Yvonne was extending herself to him as best she could? And why couldn't Yvonne see that Ford felt responsible for Lincoln's death? Knowing he was adopted now made him feel second-best. He loved his parents, Katie knew, but he was sure Lincoln was the boy closest to their hearts.

"No, we didn't blame you, but I can't convince

you of that.'' Yvonne's words were exactly what was needed, but she wasn't communicating any warmth. "I think you blamed yourself, Ford. Given that, how could we tell you about the adoption?"

"Who knows? You have no problem telling me now."

Her eyes flitted away.

"Why are you here?" he demanded, his voice low.

"The annual foundation event was planned so far in advance that we went ahead with it," Yvonne said in what seemed a complete non sequitur to Katie. "Since your father couldn't announce this year's allocation of funds at that time, we're having another, smaller party Saturday night where he'll announce the awards."

Ford looked downright deadly, his eyes narrowing until the pupils were nothing more than obsidian dots. "Your point?"

"I want you and Katie to be there." When Ford didn't say anything, Yvonne added, "It would mean so much to your father. Ford, this is an opportunity to show him you care about him."

Ford's lips parted in astonishment. "My opportunity? What about his?"

"Ford," Yvonne retorted, her temper rising. "Johnny Newman just called. He wanted to talk to your father about a possible out-of-court settlement. He says you're going to court, to get the trust money for the baby."

"Katie and I've got every right."

Yvonne gave Katie a long, hard, piercing stare, then shifted her gaze to her son again. "Ford, I know you better than you know yourself, and my guess is that Katie's not even involved in this decision. You don't care about the money. As far as that goes, we could work things out so that that would be available to the baby in the future, when he or she turns eighteen. Meantime, your father could put the foundation back in the black.''

"He'll never do that. He doesn't have enough business sense.''

"Then why don't you help him?'' Yvonne demanded, shaking her head in anger. "Why not help instead of hurting him?''

Nervously, Katie watched the quiver of muscle in Ford's cheek. It didn't bode well. "I'm hurting *him?* During the meeting with Gil, it was clear what I, Katie—and his coming grandchild—mean to him.''

"Do you think it's easy for me?'' Yvonne continued, her voice lowering with fury. "Your father doesn't even know I'm here, and if he did, he'd probably stop speaking to me. He's bullheaded, and frankly, Ford, you're just as bad.''

"More likely, he put you up to this.'' Ford's tone was liberally laced with cynicism. "If Katie and I don't show for this shindig, the press will suspect dissension in the ranks and start asking questions. You're hoping we'll play the happy Carrington newlyweds, and smile for the cameras.''

"You owe it to your father.''

Watching Yvonne's hand tighten on the doorknob, Katie felt confused. A line from an old novel suddenly came back to her. *The rich aren't like you and me.* Was Yvonne's purpose in coming here only to insure Katie and Ford's presence at a Carrington event? Or was she honestly attempting to facilitate a reconciliation between father and son? Slowly shaking her head, Katie admitted she was out of her league. These people didn't play on a level field. No, they played vertically, as if they were on a ladder, hitting from above or below. Just listening made her head ache.

"Why? What's in it for me?" Ford asked coolly. "Do you really expect me to keep up appearances when I'm not even a Carrington? When I've been disowned?"

Yvonne looked murderous. "You haven't been disowned. And indeed, I do."

Ford's words were icily formal. "I'm going to have to ask you to leave now."

"Very well." Stiffly, Yvonne turned, calmly opened the door, strode through it, then shut it behind her, leaving what shouldn't have been a deafening silence, but was.

Ford looked angry enough to take her apart piece by piece, so Katie decided to do the brash thing and go for understatement. With any luck, it might lighten the mood. She flashed him an apologetic smile. "Well, that definitely wasn't Jem and Gary." When Ford didn't respond, she added, "Before you take my head off, I want you to know I asked her to come inside because I was trying to help, not make things worse, okay?"

"This is my life, Katie. Don't interfere."

The words shouldn't have hurt, but they did. Without another word, she whirled and headed for the stairs. Maybe Ford really didn't want her in his life; maybe he'd really asked her to stay simply so he'd be better positioned when he took his parents to court.

Midway up the stairs, she turned, resting a hand on the smooth wood of the banister. Her head was spinning. Ten minutes ago, she'd been joking around with Ford, thinking she couldn't live without him. Now she didn't even like him.

His gaze was watchful. "Where do you think you're going?"

"Upstairs. I'd better decide what to wear to the party." She wasn't sure where the words had come from, but she wasn't sorry they got a rise out of him.

"We're not going!" he roared.

Yvonne was right, she decided, staring at him. He was as bullheaded as his father. "Don't you see that your mother came here trying to make amends? That the foundation party was only an excuse?"

He offered a derisive chuckle. "Wake up, Katie. A five-year-old could see through my mother. She came because Johnny Newman called—"

"Which means you lied to me, Ford. I told you I wasn't staying if you took your father to court."

"I said I'd think about that."

"Keep thinking," she retorted. "I'll be upstairs." Feeling sure she was right about Yvonne wanting to make amends, Katie took a deep breath and added, "And think about this. I love a good party. Before the last one, I'd never had caviar, and I think I'd like to sample some more."

He didn't look amused. "Katie," he warned simply.

"Heaven only knows how much havoc I can wreak this time," she continued, "without someone there to keep me in check."

"If that's supposed to be a threat, it's not going to

work." Sighing, he raked a frustrated hand through his hair and glanced away. "Please," he added, his eyes finding hers again. "I appreciate what you're trying to do here. I know how you feel about families...."

"They're the most important thing in the world." Her voice lowered, becoming solemn, and her heart caught with the hope that maybe he was coming around to her point of view. "Two working parents aren't enough. Our baby needs its grandparents. Needs...your parents."

He stared up the steps. "Damn it, Katie, why can't you leave well enough alone? The way things stand, how can I go to their party?"

"Just go," she urged. "Let's see what happens. Maybe your dad will make some sort of effort."

"Why are you doing this to me?"

Probably because she did believe so strongly in families. Life was too cold and cruel to get along without them. Besides, under Ford's tough facade was a man who needed to repair this rift before he moved on with his life. *Before he moves on with me.* "Sorry, but I'm going with or without you, Ford."

He stared at her a long moment, then something she didn't quite trust came into those devastating eyes of his—a flicker of frustrated male awareness, maybe, or the knowledge that he had the upper hand. "On one condition."

Warily, her eyes fixed on his. "Which is?"

"I buy your dress."


"FORD, people are staring at me."

He'd been staring across the crowded room at his

father, who hadn't yet bothered to speak to him, but Ford said, "I sure am, Carrot Top." Releasing a low wolf whistle between sips of Scotch, he tried to forget about his father and trailed his gaze down the daring, burnished orange dress they'd gotten for Katie. The deep gold-orange of late-autumn leaves, it was a backless design with a dramatic neckline that plunged to Katie's waist. Just shy of scandalous, it exposed enough freckles that Ford figured the simplest game of connect the dots would land them in amazing places. A full, pleated skirt nipped her waist, hiding her rounding belly.

"But everybody else is wearing black," she whispered.

From their spot near a small, seven-piece orchestra, Ford followed her gaze around the ballroom, where tall, willowy blondes in nearly identical slinky black-sheath dresses linked arms with men in tuxedos. "You've got a point." He nodded discreetly toward some blade-thin women clustered near a punch bowl. "It looks like a funeral. And if you want my opinion, those skinny black dresses make them look like knife blades dipped in tar."

"Chocolate." Katie released a soft laugh of censure as she lifted a caviar-spread cracker from the silver tray of a passing waiter and juggled it with a champagne flute of juice. "Tar sounds awful. Like those women are about to be feathered."

"Some of them probably deserve it," he volleyed, feeling far more interested in Katie, who was biting into the cracker, her moist, orange-lipsticked lips parting, the point of her tongue flickering.

"You know," she announced, "fish eggs aren't that bad if you pretend they're something else."

"Pretend," he echoed. As mad as he still was about Katie involving herself in his family affairs and pushing him to come here, he wanted to pretend only one thing, that they'd share a bed tonight. The first instant he'd seen her in the dress, he'd known his days of playing the gentleman were over. One too many nights, she'd left him burning. The nights kept lengthening and narrowing. Each was nothing more than the tantalizing shaft of light in his cracked bedroom door where he kept willing her to appear.

"I know that clerk gave us a lesson in physics," he said, his groin flexing, his attention settling where an outer layer of gossamer fabric promised to reveal the cream of breasts, only to be thwarted by a Lycra underlayer that kept her from being exposed, "but I'm still not sure how that dress stays on, Katie."

"Just barely," she whispered, her shoulders shaking with laughter as she balanced the champagne flute on a cocktail napkin, trying to look dignified. "That's how. One breath, and it would fall off."

"I'll quit holding mine, then."

"Thanks. That's what I need. To be standing here naked."

"I wouldn't mind at all." Her red hair should have clashed with the dress, but it worked in a way that was entirely Katie, just like the diamond chip she wore high on the rim of her ear. Reaching, suddenly not caring that they were in public, he flicked a finger under a shoulder strap, blowing a tuft of breath over her collarbone. "I'll huff and I'll puff..."

She blushed, looking pleased. "You're such a wolf."

"So, you remember?"

"I do," she said, her soft voice full of promise.

"You'd bring it out in any man." She was definitely collecting her share of discreet but nevertheless lusty stares. Knocking back all but the last of his Scotch, Ford felt it burn a hot trail down his throat, then slam his gut with the same kind of warmth Katie stirred. Licking his lips, he enjoyed the sting of the strong alcohol, but only because he so badly wanted to taste something so much stronger…her. "Not many women could get away with that dress, Carrot Top."

She shot him a nervous smile. "I'm not sure I am."

"You carry it off like a dream." But what was beneath? he wondered. A barely there thong or hand-sewn garter belt with lace as soft as water? Feeling unsettled, Ford rattled the ice in his glass, then knocked back another swallow.

She was smiling. "I had fun shopping for the dress."

"Me, too."

Once he'd put aside his anger, they'd had a blast. In addition to buying the dress, he'd pulled her into children's departments, and they'd argued over everything from cribs to diaper bags and strollers.

"The party's definitely smaller than the last," Katie commented.

Somehow, that ruffled his pride. Why, he didn't know. He told himself he'd let the foundation go belly up before he'd step in and straighten it out. He wasn't even a Carrington. His birthright, like his marriage, he thought with sudden annoyance, was a sham. An in-name-only deal. Tonight proved it. When they got home, Katie would sleep alone, as usual. Here, his mother's air kisses and his father's avoidance showed neither was seeking a reconciliation, after all. Staring into the bottom of his glass, Ford abruptly decided there was another sip left and downed it. Not that he felt it. He never did. He could drink all night and still be rock steady.

*Too bad.* Tonight, he wouldn't mind enjoying the luxury of getting a little high. He resented being here, especially since his and Katie's presence was so obviously calculated to assure people that the Carringtons were a unified force. More than ever, his resolve to take his parents to court strengthened. He didn't care what Katie said. Maybe he'd feel differently if his father had asked for his help with the foundation. Or if his parents had broken the news of his adoption some other way. Or if they'd offered some sign tonight that they cared for him. But they hadn't.

Glancing around again, he considered leaving, but Katie looked so excited in her new dress that he simply couldn't. Fortunately, she was too good-hearted to even notice how Blane rallied the women around herself this evening. She'd had no claim on Ford before his marriage, but she was making sure Katie got snubbed. Needing something to lighten his mood, he said, "C'mon, let's dance." Taking her drink, he set it on a tray, along with his Scotch, then grasped her hand and headed for a space in front of the orchestra.

Katie hung back, mortified. "Ford, I can't!"

"If you railroaded me into coming here," he assured her, catching a glimpse of his parents out of the corner of his eye, "you can do anything, Katie."

Under her breath, she protested, "I didn't exactly have dancing lessons when I was a kid, Ford."

He chuckled. "I saw you cutting a rug in the back of Jem's truck after the team penning events."

"Oh, kiss my round Irish behind," she muttered. "Dancing to Conway Twitty's different."

"Now, be a good Irish lass," he murmured, leaving her just long enough to whisper to the orchestra leader. Returning, he said, "I requested our song."

She looked furious. "We don't have a song."

Pulling her close, he caught one of her hands, curled it over his shoulder, then twined their fingers. Bending close, he stroked her cheek with his. "We do now, Carrot Top."

"'Orange Blossom Special'!" she exclaimed when the orchestra broke into the bluegrass tune. Delighted, she laughed with him as he stepped away, and they danced in circles around each other, clapping their hands. Stomping silk-covered high heels on the floor, she encouraged the staid crowd until whoops, hoots and hollers began to sound. By the time the ditty was ending, the floor was vibrating. Wrapping an arm behind her back, Ford suddenly drew her flush against him. He spun her, then dipped her so low that her head almost touched the floor.

"Ford!" she squealed.

Staring down, he took in the mouthwatering bare strip of skin between her breasts, then her shapely hips, over which he so desperately wanted to mold his hands. When his gaze settled on the full skirt that hid the tummy rounding with their baby, he felt weak.

To hell with his parents. Who gave a damn that they'd cut him so deeply tonight? All that mattered was Katie and the baby. He brought her up, and when she found her footing, his mouth closed—simply, ravenously—over hers. Only vaguely aware of the soft ahs voiced by romantics in the crowd, he deepened a kiss that left him hot, straining against her and shuddering. Knowing he had to break it off, he led Katie from the floor, feeling so unsteady that he barely realized he'd stopped in front of Blane. The unkind way her eyes flickered over Katie made Ford's already warm blood rise.

"I can see you're quite accomplished, Katie," Blane said.

Flushed from their kiss, her eyes bright, Katie wasn't ready for the assault Ford saw coming. Possessively, he slipped his arm around her waist. "Blane," he warned.

But it was too late. Just as cameras moved in on the three of them, Blane whispered, "Mark my words. She'll never be a true Carrington."

Glad Katie hadn't heard, Ford was dangerously tempted to divulge the truth. *He* wasn't a Carrington, either. "She's my wife," he informed Blane, a strangely possessive feeling moving through him as he spoke the words. "She's already a Carrington. Everyone here sees her charm."

The society column reporters were crowding around her, and he watched with a mixture of pride and amusement as Katie gamely answered even their most ludicrous questions.

"Katie, who does your hair?"

"A guy named Billy Jones. He lives downstairs in

my old building, and he works out of his apartment.''
Her bubbling laughter grew deeper. ''He charges
seven bucks.'' With a wicked glint in her eyes, she
added, ''But I bet if you print this, his prices will go
up after tonight.''

The reporters loved her. Who wouldn't? It was just
like Katie to use a moment in the spotlight to give a
friend an endorsement. Unfortunately, Blane edged
next to her. ''Let's use this publicity to get to the
important issues,'' Blane said, lightly chastising Katie
as if she were acting frivolously.

Ford sighed. It was a catch-22. If he didn't step in,
Blane might eat Katie alive. If he did, it would appear
that Katie couldn't handle herself. His mouth set in a
grim line, his eyes turning watchful as he listened to
Blane try to subtly sabotage Katie in front of the media. Trouble was, Blane went too far. She hinted that
a woman raised on a farm could never understand the
full nature of what the Carrington Foundation was
trying to accomplish. As she dug herself in deeper
with every word, Ford began to wonder if Katie
wasn't intentionally giving Blane enough rope to
hang herself by. It was hard to tell.

''I'm afraid I must correct you, Blane,'' Katie said
at last. ''Money and status never save human lives,
only other people can.''

''Of course,'' agreed Blane. ''Well put. And in
Austin, I'm proud to say my family has been to the
law what the Carringtons have been to medicine. Until recently, there *was* talk of merging the Gilcrest
Endowment with the Carrington Foundation....''

Great. For those who had ears to hear, Blane was
implying that the deal had been contingent on her

relationship with Ford. As she rambled on about projects such as the Carrington Clinic, which she said would be unable to open its doors tomorrow as planned, Ford found himself hoping that Katie would realize Blane was a thwarted daddy's girl. She was sore about Katie's marriage, and now, behind the scenes, she was trying to upset a deal between her family and Ford's. While an association with the Gilcrest Endowment could replenish the Carrington Foundation's coffers, neither family was fool enough to rest a business deal on a love affair. But Blane's ego was bruised, and she'd do whatever she could to dissuade the Gilcrests.

When Katie placed her hand on Blane's arm as if for support, Ford's lips parted in unspoken warning. "And to think I was rambling on about my hair," Katie murmured, looking stricken, and making Ford think she'd walked right into Blane's trap. "Blane's so right," Katie continued, shaking her head with worry. "Can you please print something?" Katie glanced around, her eyes settling on the orchestra members, who were rising to take a break. "Wait a minute." Firmly grasping Blane's hand, Katie strode across the floor and stopped in front of a microphone David Carrington had used earlier to announce the annual allocations.

"Can everybody hear me? You in the back? Can you hear?" Taking a deep breath and hooking an arm around Blane's waist in a show of solidarity, Katie spoke clearly into the microphone, repeating everything Blane had said, emphasizing Carrington-funded projects that were in jeopardy.

Blane looked fit to kill. But Katie's beautiful green

eyes were alive with passion, and Ford had never heard a voice so earnest. "All my life, I've been aware of the Carrington Foundation, as have so many very grateful people in Austin. Tomorrow, the Carrington Clinic was supposed to open its doors at eight a.m., but according to a very concerned Blane Gilcrest, that opening has been postponed!"

Ford sighed with frustration. If the foundation had watched its investments more carefully, this would never have happened. Apparently the new clinic had gone over budget, and Ford's father had decided to put it on the back burner in favor of other projects. Too bad. New legislation had been implemented that would allow the clinic to run with a volunteer staff and accept donations from pharmacies.

"So," Katie was saying, "I lay down a challenge to my co-workers at Maitland Maternity who, like Dr. Ford Carrington and I, are off work tomorrow. We'll be at the Carrington Clinic building bright and early. If you're in need of free medical attention, I promise we'll do whatever we can."

Blane smiled falsely. "I'll certainly be there!"

Katie grinned. "Of course you will. It was your idea, after all."

Despite the fact Katie had just roped him even further into Carrington business, Ford chuckled. As she strode to his side again, he slid his hands around her waist; her buttocks nestled against his groin, shooting white heat through his limbs. Grinning wickedly at him, she whispered, "Blane was just awful to me the last time I met her. But I think she might be warming to me now. What do you think?"

No doubt, Blane had fled for the bathroom, where

she was probably pacing and fuming, scheming to get Katie back at the Carrington Clinic tomorrow. "Seeing the two of you at the microphone together, given what happened at the last party, was…" Ford smiled, then said, "Strangely perfect. I think you've got Blane under control, Katie."

She laughed. "Now I need to work on you."

His eyes held hers, and the troubles with his family receded. "What have you got in mind?" he asked throatily. "Light bondage, so I can't get away?"

"Keep talking dirty and you won't get a kiss goodnight."

"When I get you home, Katie," he warned, "I'm not planning on doing any talking at all."

# CHAPTER EIGHT

SHRUGGING out of his jacket, Ford watched as Katie flicked on the dim track lights over the sink, opened the refrigerator door and bent, scrutinizing the lower shelves. He draped the jacket around the back of a chair and seated himself at the kitchen table, groaning as he yanked the knot of his tie. "I hate ties," he complained.

Glancing over her shoulder, Katie offered her quick once-over. "So, that's why you really became a doctor, huh?" she teased. "Stethoscopes don't pinch as much?"

With his hands clasped behind his neck, he leaned back, balancing the chair on its back legs and surveying Katie, who was still standing in a glowing wedge of light from the refrigerator. He shook his head. "Nothing could pinch more than the noose I felt I had around my neck at that damn party."

She looked hurt. "We had a good time, Ford."

"Yeah. I take it back. We did." The undercurrents with his family had ruined it for him, though, not that he'd tell Katie when she'd had such a good time. He could still hear his mother, offering idle chitchat as if they hadn't parted on bad terms just a week ago, and he could see his father shaking hands and grinning, talking to each guest—except Ford and Katie—as if they were all his best friends. Oh, after Ford's mother had dropped by, he'd considered calling Johnny Newman again and telling him to drop the proceedings. But not now, not when he'd humbled himself by going to the party, only to be treated like a pariah. Abruptly bringing down the chair legs, Ford agitatedly kicked off his shoes and removed his cuff links. With a toss he threw them onto the table and rolled up his sleeves.

Katie hauled a plastic bowl to the countertop. "Is a sandwich okay?"

"Leftover pimento cheese?" he asked, his mouth suddenly watering for it. The trick, Katie had explained, was freezing Velveeta so it could be grated. After that she'd added Cracker Barrel cheese and stirred in sugar with mayonnaise, pimentos and hot chili peppers. A slight smile curled his lips. Before Katie moved in, he'd never guessed he'd enjoy eating at home with a partner. Most women he knew didn't cook and liked to dine out.

She was frowning thoughtfully. "And maybe some potato chips?"

"That'd be great," he said.

Katie headed for the bread box, lifting a hand to smooth the red-gold waves of her hair. Against the drab, stainless steel backdrop of the kitchen, her dress looked like a burst of orange sun; under the track lights, it reflected on skin that was otherwise as white as clouds. "Too bad you've volunteered us for work tomorrow at the clinic," he said, hoping his parents wouldn't turn up there. "We could have spent the day together."

"And tomorrow night's out. I'm on night shift."

Ford nodded. "I'm on call."

"The hospital probably won't need you. Maybe you should stop by and see Jem and Gary. They're still teaching that mare to load in the trailer, and they could use an extra hand."

"When they came for dinner, I said I'd help."

Katie nodded absently, as if his growing relationship with her brothers was the most natural thing in the world. Deep down, Ford marveled at it. Marveled, too, that he liked the life he and Katie were slowly, silently building, how they were becoming part of each other's lives. After a long moment, she dropped a loaf of bread, spring water and two paper towels on the table. She quirked an eyebrow. "A penny?"

He shrugged. "I like coming home with you, Katie." He enjoyed this quiet, relaxed domesticity.

She shook her head. "How could you ever live in this huge house alone?"

He shrugged. "No idea." Opening the bread bag, he counted out four slices, then frowned. "Didn't you get enough to eat at the party?"

"Caviar isn't the most filling food, I discovered. Maybe next time, your mama should give us the whole fish instead of just the eggs."

He chuckled, then sobered, thinking of his mother, the smile not quite meeting his eyes. "My thoughts exactly."

Katie stopped in front of him, her hands on her hips, her freshly manicured fingers flared, their tips painted to match the orange dress. She smiled in a way that made Ford want to call her countless outmoded, sexually charged names such as vixen and wanton. "Besides, Ford, we are eating for two."

The words tugged at his heart, turning his breath shallow. He was a doctor, well-versed in anatomy and the fine art of reproduction, but still, he could barely believe it. *Our baby. Growing inside you, Katie. Right now.* Drawing a deep breath, he slipped a hand easily over hers and pulled her close. "What is this, anyway?" he murmured, grasping a handful of material near her waist. "Chiffon? Silk? Tulle? Did the clerk ever tell us?"

Katie's voice was strangely unsteady. "I don't remember her saying, Ford."

"And you're wearing that dangerous perfume again."

Her brows crinkled. "What perfume?"

"Soap and water." He smiled into wicked eyes that were as clear as lake water. "Your scent," he added huskily. "It drives me wild, Katie." When he tightened his fingers on her waist, slowly rubbing his thumbs on the belly that held their child, she came a half step nearer. *Our baby. Parts of me and Katie. Belonging to us both.* "Hope he has your eyes, Katie."

"She," Katie countered. "Hope she has yours."

"Hmm. Hope she has red hair then."

Her smile broadened. "Odds are against it. Don't they teach you doctors anything about recessive genes? I bet his hair's black."

"Her," corrected Ford. "Which means no freckles," he added, his tone low, his eyes raking where her neckline plunged to her waist, leaving a bare strip of freckled skin. "And freckles are so nice, Katie, especially yours." Leaning forward, he pressed a damp, searing kiss between her ribs. She gave a shudder that moved through his body, stirring want so deep that it could have come from inside his bones. Something—Katie's eyes, her mouth, her smile—pulled his gaze to hers again, and he wordlessly urged her to turn, drawing her between his legs, settling her high on his thigh.

Twisting toward him, she made a soft embarrassed sound, not quite a chuckle. "There's no room for the dress."

With a surreptitious breath, he spread his legs wider, making space, but because the movement fully opened him to her, the rustling press of fabric suddenly felt too acute against his groin. *Feathery*, he thought. *Agonizing*.

"Ready for your sandwich?" she said.

His eyes settled where the looser, outer fabric of the neckline gaped away from the tighter fabric beneath that cupped her breasts. "A sandwich?" His voice caught, turning throaty and gruff. "I can think of things I want more."

Her eyes were mischievous. "Be good and maybe you'll get lucky."

He offered a slow smile. "Tease," he accused.

"Teasing might be the only real power women have, Ford."

His shoulders shook with a suppressed chuckle. "Somehow, it's hard to construe you as the weaker sex, Katie."

Plucking a knife from where she'd left it in the pimento cheese, she waved it in his direction. "Be careful what you say about me, Ford."

He pretended to consider. "I wouldn't waste a potential murder weapon on me. You may need it tomorrow when you see Blane at the clinic.''

"I already told you," Katie returned. "Blane's warming to me." Handing him a sandwich, Katie turned so she nearly faced him, and while they ate in silence, his eyes flickered over her. Eyeliner and a light coat of mascara had deepened the color of her eyes, making her look like a relaxed, exotic jungle cat. Alluring. Timeless. Beautiful. Suddenly, she frowned, taking in the neat half-moon of her bite marks. "Lipstick on my bread."

"You'd better eat it off before I do."

Chuckling, she made a point of quickly polishing off the sandwich, washing down the last bite with spring water. Dusting her hands over a paper towel, she looked at him with solemnity. "I don't want to think you're right, Ford," she began tentatively. "I mean, about your mother wanting us at the party only for show." She gave a short sigh. "Look, are you okay?"

"Okay?"

She tilted her head in a way that was purely female, her pursed, damp lips pulled into a lopsided frown. "I really thought your mother came here to make amends, and that when you acted so testily—"

"No act. I *was* testy."

"When you weren't receptive to her, I thought she decided to use the foundation as an excuse for coming here."

His voice hardened. "I doubt it, given the fact that she barely spoke to us tonight and only when other people were around."

Honesty shone in her eyes. "I'm sorry I forced you to go."

"I'm a big boy. You can't force me to do anything."

"Well...she did have a lot of guests."

"C'mon, don't make excuses. My father didn't even say hello." Ford's lips drew into a thin, uncompromising line. "Look," he added after a moment. "I'm sorry. But where they're concerned, I have to be hard. I've wanted to protect you. I haven't wanted you drawn into my family's mess, not even this far."

He didn't completely understand the hurt that crossed her features until she said, "But right now, they're my family, too, Ford. I mean...while we're still married."

Her quiet way of saying the words touched him. Family—even a temporary one—meant everything to Katie. Maybe to him, too. Had Lincoln lived, maybe Ford and his brother would have become as close as Jem and Gary. Ford wanted to think so.

"I don't know if I could...ever live like that," added Katie.

His arms encircled her waist, squeezing tight. "Like what?"

"Interacting with people when there's that much tension, for one." She winced. "And smiling publicly when things are so bad behind closed doors. I even felt kind of strange dancing with you," she admitted, her voice going suddenly soft, her eyes tracing his mouth and lingering a second too long. "Kissing you publicly didn't feel right...not when I know they don't approve of the relationship."

"It's me they don't approve of."

"I can't believe that." Something fierce touched her voice. "Your mother told me she's happy about the baby, and I believe her. She was crying in your father's study, too. She's torn, Ford. And your father loves you. How could he not? He just can't show it. It's so unnecessary," she added, the words touched with angry vehemence. "So unloving."

A second passed. He realized he was holding his breath, and exhaled slowly. "Love—" His voice was hoarse. "Is that what you're looking for here, Katie?"

Emotion caught in her throat. "Aren't you?"

"I'm not even sure I know what love is."

Her lovely green eyes looked cloudy, disturbed. "It's what happens when everybody puts aside their differences and pulls together."

"No chance of that with my family, Katie."

"If you take them to court," she said in what was almost a whisper, "you'll make sure you never reconcile."

His one word was hard. "So?"

"Don't do it. For me, Ford."

Just moments ago, he'd decided he was definitely going to court, but as far as Katie was concerned, that would strip her and the baby of extended family. "For you?" he found himself saying, "All right, Katie." His eyes lowered, trailing to her waist in tandem with a finger; slowly he traced a tantalizing line all the way down, then up again, pausing between her breasts. "Katie," he murmured, her name coming with a soft pant that turned his lips dry.

"What?"

"Nothing," he whispered. "Just Katie."

Her breasts were full, ripe as summer fruit, breathtaking. He inched a finger under the soft outer fabric of the dress, the way he'd wanted to all night, then he splayed his whole hand on the stretchy fabric beneath, gliding his palm over a plump mound, lifting it high with his first caress, his fingers folding to cup her. She shuddered as he squeezed, his thumb and finger rolling a constricted tip as his mouth found hers. His mind turned sluggish, and his groin thickened, feeling almost painfully heavy, pressuring the zipper of his slacks. "Right now, I feel like I could never get enough of this," he said with a ragged sigh of need. "Enough of you. It's time we started sleeping together, Katie. Every night. Let's give it a try."

Her breath caught. "I like the idea of that."

He simply nodded, needing the connection he'd felt the night they made their baby. His eyes never leaving her face, he slid his hand under the tight stretchy fabric of the dress so he could touch her bare breast.

"Oh, Ford," she whimpered, either her voice or the touch making heat eddy in his belly. He drew a sharp breath and inhaled the musky scent of her, a scent that haunted him night after night when he lay awake, hard and hurting and imagining her. "Every night, I've been hoping you'd come to my bed. Please, Katie. I can't stand it anymore."

Gently, she cupped his face. "Me, neither," she whispered, and then she offered herself by closing her mouth over his.

THEY WOUND UP in her bed, not his, and vaguely Katie wondered if Ford had anticipated this scene of seduction long ago. There were other guest rooms, after all. Rooms without thick, toe-melting carpet, red satin sheets and moonlight. But Ford had put her here, where she'd lain awake so many nights fantasizing about him.

Breathlessly, she lay back on the high, firm mattress, nestling her head deeply into a pile of tapestried pillows, the full skirt of her dress flaring over the bedspread. Her heart was hammering so hard that she felt she couldn't speak, so she didn't even try. From outside, moonlight streamed between the open curtains, shining onto the gauzy white canopy above her, and when Ford shrugged from his pressed dress shirt, that same moonlight caught in the dark, tangled hair covering his chest, turning it silver. As he edged a knee onto the mattress, she sucked in a breath, whispering, "The moon…it's like a dream, Ford."

"You're a dream."

Hot and strained, his voice spoke of his need for release, and when her smoky gaze dropped to his slacks, her whole body tightened, every nerve as taut as wire, her insides jumpy. The outline of him was hard, promising. "A dream," she whispered. "But we're real, Ford." And after this, their marriage would be, too.

"I know." Gently hooking his fingers under the heels of her shoes, he slid them off, letting them drop over the sides of the bed, then he cupped her insteps, his massaging palms warm through her stockings, but not nearly as warm as the blood pulsing through her veins.

She'd known the promise of sex with him would be too much to deny. Too many fantasies had fueled the passion that led her to his bed in September. Her dreams had paled by comparison, and since then, living under the same roof had turned longing into torture. Gasping, she felt his two strong, broad hands steal under the dress, across her bare skin to cup her shoulders.

Everything went utterly still, then his breath caught audibly. So much blood rushed in her ears that she barely heard. Wordlessly, moaning softly, he pushed the dress from her shoulders, sliding the fabric along her arms, baring her breasts as he eased the bodice to her waist.

Chill winter air hit her. Right before she felt the summer heat of his mouth, her nipples puckered. Tunneling her hands deeply into the silken, dark midnight of his hair, she arched wantonly, the bold, swirling thrust of his tongue shooting curling heat through her loosening limbs. He, too, had fantasized. With his every movement, she could feel his nights of need, nights where he'd lain awake, aroused and frustrated, his sleepless, feverish mind concocting ways to please her.

Suckling her, he rolled a taut nipple around his silken tongue, then he whispered, "Every night, I'm aware of you just down the hall, Katie. I kept thinking you'd come to me. I've wanted...." His voice dropped, too guttural with desire to understand, his fiery mouth otherwise engaged.

"I know you're down the hall," she whimpered, her lower body straining. "The night you were riding, I thought you might come...."

A hoarse rasp blew across her breast. "We're here now, Katie." His thighs pressed apart her legs, his searing mouth making her writhe. When it touched a beaded nipple, it felt so slow and delicious that she thought she'd die from thwarted need. Feeling perspiration slick her skin, she suddenly remembered how, months ago, his fingers had stroked her intimately, and she braced herself for the powerful feel of a penetration she'd never forgotten. Lifting her hips, she sought him once more, wishing scads of pleated fabric weren't still between them.

"Ford..." Her breath fitful, she swiftly shifted enough to release her side zipper. But he was still kneading her breast, his low moan of pleasure coming with the arduous strokes of his tongue, and before she knew what was happening, she was mindlessly pushing her hands into his hair another time, longing for his molten tongue, reveling in how the silken strands of his hair fell between her fingers and how his hard, throbbing heat worried her thigh.

*We're married.* It hit her with renewed force as her hands slid hungrily from his hair down the rippling muscles of his back. Pressing her thighs together, she whimpered. Didn't he know he was pulling her apart?

Relief shot through her when a hand rustled under the unwanted mountain of fabric. Firm and strong, it glided slowly along the inside of her thigh, displacing material. Pulling down her hose. Pulling down her best panties.

And then he found her. Uttering a sharp cry at the touch, she felt tears sting her eyes. She'd wanted him too much, too long. When he pulled the panties again, just a shred of lace around her thighs, she could feel how badly she wanted him. Panting, he slipped them over her feet. Then the dress was gone, bunched beside her on the bed.

"Oh, Katie," he whispered.

"Yes?"

His hand slid over her belly, making the flesh quiver. "We made a baby, Katie," he whispered simply, lying fully on top of her.

"Yes, we did," she whispered.

And then the room burst. The flesh of her thighs leaped, then her heart thundered as he found her cleft, gingerly parting the sides and slowly pushing in two fingers. Everything inside her exploded. Their scent filled the room. His fingers penetrated more deeply than she could bear, a thumb circling the nub as he made a sound so male and sexual that she shuddered.

A second later, he'd stripped off his slacks, and she watched him breathlessly, taking in his dark, steamily glazed eyes, the devilish angles of his face, the wild hair coating his body, settling her gaze where his arousal thrust from a tangle of coarse hair. Sucking a slow breath through clenched teeth, he lay atop her again, his mouth finding hers, his hand fondling her breast.

"I want more," she whispered. She wanted him against her womb. She wanted never to leave this house. She wanted her papa to like him, and for his parents to love him. And then suddenly, those thoughts turned fuzzy, and her hips were straining again, grasping for pleasure only this man could give.

He tossed the dress from the mattress. It hit the air like a wild sunburst in the sky of the room. The stockings followed, floating like wisps of skywriting, the message lost to passion. Shifting her, he stripped down the spread, so they lay on red satin.

Naked, she felt him then, burning and ready between her legs, and a sharp, almost animal cry

brought her to him. His voice was guttural. "Here…"
Reaching, he grasped a pillow, the threads rasping her
backside as he slid it beneath her. Silk tassels stroked
the backs of her thighs, then suddenly, he plunged.
Fast, hard, deep, he pulled another cry from her, and
another. Each time, the raised tilt of her hips forced
him deeper.

The climax was a wave. Hers, sweeping, rippling
shivers. His, cresting then shuddering with after-
shocks. He was throbbing and pressed to her womb,
touching their child, when he whispered, "I'm in love
with you, Katie. I think I've been in love with you
for a long time."

## CHAPTER NINE

"JEM? GARY?" Ford called the next evening as he swung open the door at the Toppers' farmhouse. "Anybody home?" He stared down the hallway, surprised not to see Katie's brothers. Katie was working tonight, and Ford had called ahead so they'd expect him. *Katie,* Ford thought with a pensive sigh. Last night was a mixed blessing. He was in love with her. But he'd lied. He wasn't giving up his legal case. He couldn't. Today, he and Katie had seen his parents at the clinic, and they hadn't been any more receptive than at the party. Ford wanted—and deserved—good, old-fashioned Texas revenge. High noon. The court scene. The whole works.

Did that mean his feelings for Katie didn't run deep enough to make a loving, lasting marriage out of what was going on between them? Wasn't he a good enough man to lay aside the past and make amends that would carry him and his father into a future that would suit Katie? God knew, Ford hadn't known much warmth growing up. Did that mean Katie needed things he'd never be able to give? Pushing aside such thoughts, Ford stepped across the threshold, lifting his voice as he headed down the hallway. "Jem? Gary?" His glance took in a braided rug and plaid-upholstered couch in the living room, then some equestrian statues on top of the TV. He frowned. Maybe Jem and Gary were already at the horse trailer, which they kept parked by the barn.

Starting to feel like an intruder, Ford peered through the living room doorway into the kitchen, just in time to see a big, burly man who had to be Jack Topper whirl at the kitchen sink. He was well over six feet, his massive shoulders pulling at the seams of the down vest he wore over a blue flannel shirt. A shock of thick, dark red hair fell onto a wrinkled forehead, and blue eyes blazed from a broad face that didn't at all resemble Katie's. His fingers slowly crept across the counter, curling around a steaming coffee mug as if he was considering using it as a weapon. "Who are you?" Jack drew a sharp breath. "Oh," he added quickly. "Bet you're Katie's husband. I just got home from Dallas a couple minutes ago. Gary and Jem told me...."

"Yeah," Ford managed to say as Jack's sky blue eyes narrowed, drifting down his leather jacket, chambray work shirt and jeans to fancy cowboy boots. "It's nice to meet you, Mr. Topper. I know this must come as a surprise, but I'm Ford Carrington—"

Ford stopped midsentence, seeing that the words were hardly having the desired effect. Jack paled, then clutched his heart. Instinctively, Ford took a step closer, checking Jack's coloring, fearing the man was having a heart attack.

Jack gasped. "*You're* her husband?"

Rushing into an explanation, Ford left nothing out except the pregnancy. "You weren't supposed to hear about it this way. Jem and Gary promised they'd let Katie and me tell you. We thought you were coming back tomorrow, and since Katie's working night shift, I just came over to help load a mare into the trailer—''

''Jem and Gary started to tell me who—'' Jack choked on his words, then rambled on. ''I didn't let them finish. I came inside to call Katie. If she's got something to say to me, she'd better tell me herself. But...not you. Not this. She's David Carrington's, don't you understand? Dear God, she's his. *His*. Me and Millie should have told him.... Oh, Lord in heaven, no. My baby girl couldn't have done this, couldn't have married you. It's the sins of the devil being visited upon us. I should have known.''

Ford had heard Jack Topper was religious, but seeing Katie's marriage as a sin definitely seemed an overreaction. In fact, the whole point was that she and Ford *weren't* living in sin. But it was something Jack had said earlier that niggled. ''She's David Carrington's? What do you mean by that?'' Why had Jack mentioned Ford's father's name?

Jack's lips parted in horror; it was as if he wasn't staring at Ford at all, but at the devil incarnate. His words as scratchy as sandpaper, he said, ''You're Ford...Ford *Carrington*, boy? You did say Carrington? Carrington's your last name?''

This whole production was so strange that Ford had no idea what to say, but it was clear that Ford's being a Carrington went into the minus column for Jack Topper. ''If you must know,'' Ford said, feeling awkward divulging the information, but hoping it would help, ''I'm adopted. So, from a biological standpoint...''

Relief flooded the man's face, and yet his large

body seemed to weaken. He sagged against the counter as if he'd just aged thirty years. "You're the older one then?"

Older one? Why would Katie's father know anything about Lincoln? And why was he so familiar with Ford's family? Ford took another step into the kitchen. "I don't know what's going on here, Mr. Topper, but I'm sorry I gave you such a start." He extended a hand, which Katie's father shook weakly. "I don't know what I've said to upset you, Mr. Topper. Katie and I planned to have you over for dinner. We wanted to do this right."

Jack looked shaken. "No problem. You can call me Jack." Lifting the coffee cup, the older man took a few lumbering steps to an island countertop, sat down and then heaved out a breath so long that he could have been holding it since the day the Creator separated heaven and earth.

Frowning, Ford circled the island and sat opposite him. He stared at Jack hard, the way he did patients when he was operating, then grabbed the topic with the tenacity of a pit bull. "Now, what did you mean? About David Carrington?"

Jack suddenly looked as if he'd rather be anywhere in the world but in his kitchen with Ford. "Nothing. And anyway, you're adopted. That's what you said, right?"

Ford frowned. "What do you know about my family?"

Jack eyed the man who'd married his daughter. "Nothing."

"Right," Ford muttered, not about to leave this kitchen until he knew what was afoot. Using every skill he'd learned during his upbringing, including base flattery and obsequious charm, he assured Jack he'd find out the connection between the families if Jack wouldn't tell him, then he named countless local private investigators who'd be happy to work for him. Only when he added that he was estranged from his family, anyway, did Jack's tongue loosen, compassion overtaking his broad, plain, good-hearted features. Even as he talked, making Ford's world come unhinged for the second time in the past few weeks, Ford got the sense that the man's motive was to repair family ties. Just like Katie, Jack Topper seemed to want to mend the rift between Ford and his father.

"What?" Ford murmured when Jack finished telling his story. "I just don't believe it."

"Maybe you'll like your folks better now," said Jack. "Besides, the way things sit with you and Katie, it don't seem right for you two not to know, though I don't know how my baby girl's gonna take the news. The boys told me she got married, but I had no idea it was to a Carrington." Hooking beefy fingers around the mug handle, Jack took a deep gulp of coffee.

Ford was shaken. "Mind if I get a cup?"

"Help yourself, boy."

Ford poured himself some coffee, circled the island and seated himself. Drinking it half down, he wished it was something stronger, aged whiskey that would curl in a warm knot in his stomach, maybe. He took the deepest breath of his life. "This throws a wrench in things."

"Well, every word is true," Jack said with a sigh.

"I don't know what we're going to do about Katie. Or your papa. He doesn't know."

With the words, another strange, fundamental shift occurred, a huge reversal, and Ford suddenly thought of how the *Titanic* probably looked when it upended, turning slowly on its stern and then plunging to the bottom of the Atlantic. Once more, he reviewed Jack's speech in his mind, and he recalled Katie telling him about her mother's nursing career, how she'd said it had inspired her to become a nurse.

What Katie didn't know was that Millie Topper, then Millie McDean, had been working at Texas General Hospital on David Carrington's surgical team, and that, despite David's marriage, a relationship had evolved, an extramarital affair during which Katie was conceived.

It was more than Ford could process. "My father's really her father..." Why, just when you thought everything might turn out fine, did zingers like this come along?

"It was nobody's fault, mind you," Jack said quickly, looking torn between maintaining his silence and telling the rest of the story. Clearly, he wanted to set things right so Ford would forgive his parents. "Not your mama's. Nor your papa's. But before your little brother was born..."

"What do you know about Lincoln?"

"Nothing more than your mama finally got pregnant with a baby boy after you were adopted. We never talked about the family...about you, after that. Hell, I guess I made a point of not following the society news." Jack paused, suddenly glancing through a window with a faraway look that suggested he was remembering the wife he'd lost, so Ford didn't apprise him of Lincoln's death. "You know," Jack continued, looking at Ford again, "it was really tough between your folks at that time."

"Like I said, my parents and I aren't close." Ford's voice lowered, coming out more gruffly than he'd intended. "If you want the truth, I'm not even sure I'll ever speak to my father again." *At least not outside a court of law.* "So, it doesn't matter if you tell me everything else you know." Convincing himself the lump in his throat wasn't emotion, Ford swallowed it, his eyes not moving from Jack's. "I want to know everything," he repeated.

As Jack surveyed him, he seemed somehow older to Ford, as if he'd seen too much of the world. A slight smile touched his lips when Jem and Gary appeared in the distance, coming from the barn. Ford followed his gaze just as the late afternoon sun peeked from behind thick clouds that threatened rain. If all this was true—something Ford meant to find out—then everything had changed. Hell, if David was Katie's biological father, Katie had legal rights to the baby's trust fund. She was a blood Carrington. The money was hers. Unbelievable. Ford wouldn't even have to take them to court. But taking the money would break the foundation.

"You really don't get along with your papa, boy?" Jack said.

*Papa?* Ford couldn't imagine calling his father that, but under Jack's gaze, Ford admitted to himself that, no matter what he called David, the man's rejection hurt. He said nothing, only nodded, taking another sip of coffee as he stared toward the field where the horses ran.

"Surprised to hear it. Millie—that's my wife, Katie's mama—she said David wanted kids real bad. So bad he could taste it. That's what Millie said." Biting his lip, Jack shook his head as if they'd all just escaped a very close call. "For a minute there, I was scared to death. I thought you and Katie was blood relations."

No wonder Jack had looked as if he were about to have a heart attack. Trying to tell himself they'd all laugh about this someday, Ford managed to reply, "Well, we're not."

"Thank the good Lord. And now that I've got my wits about me again, I can tell you're older than Katie." He shook his head. "I can't even believe it. You swear you're married to my baby girl?"

Ford nodded. "I sure am."

"Holy moly." Jack sighed again as if he couldn't fathom it. "Too bad you're not getting along with your folks, 'cause they wanted you bad. Your papa told Millie that before you were adopted, they'd tried to have a baby for years...."

"Really?" Ford listened with rapt attention as Jack plunged into the story once more, as if only countless retelling could convince them both of its veracity. While working at Texas General, Katie's mother had comforted David at a time when new medical treatments were being introduced, which Yvonne felt would allow her to have a child. "But your papa feared this new one was like all the other treatments they'd tried, and I guess he had to...well, do all kinds of things a man doesn't want to in order to help get her in the family way, know what I mean?''

As a doctor, Ford was well aware of what men went through when there were fertility problems, and while he hardly wanted to hear this about his parents, he was equally hungry for the information. Especially since, given the age difference between himself and Lincoln, he'd always assumed his mother had trouble conceiving. It never occurred to him that his strong, stiff-upper-lipped father had been infertile…that the man who could never humble himself to ask for any kind of help couldn't make his wife pregnant.

"He didn't feel like a man," Jack continued, the words taking on a lilting cadence, either from his Irish blood or the fact that he was a natural storyteller. "And when it seemed like this treatment wouldn't work, either, your mama got real upset."

Ford's heart tensed. He would have been seven at the time. Was that the reason for the tension he remembered? Or was he trying to rewrite history, recasting the past in a new light so he could find a way of making up with his family for Katie's sake? Katie was right, after all. Family mattered. The clutch of his heart told him so. And he was in love. He just didn't know if he could ever swallow enough pride to give her the extended family she seemed to need. If he tried, would his father meet him halfway? "My mother was upset?"

Jack nodded, and although he didn't divulge all that Millie had apparently told him years ago, Ford could read between the lines. David would have been satisfied not to try another time. "Millie said he was content to have one son to carry on the family name, but your mama wanted more babies." Jack's eyes softened. "Women do, you know."

He thought of Katie, of how her eyes glazed when they talked of their child. He thought of the possibility of having more children with her. His words sounded strangely unsteady even to his own ears. "My mother had me."

"Yeah. But maybe she thought you needed brothers and sisters. Anyhow, your papa thought trying to get pregnant would just hurt your mama, since so many treatments hadn't worked. And he had no one to talk to, except Millie, who was working with him over at Texas General. She was a wonderful woman. Warm as sunshine. Heart as big as a house. I'd only known her two months when I proposed, saying I'd be papa to her coming baby. Not that a short engagement mattered. That woman had me the first time our eyes met." Jack's gaze caught Ford's. "I want you to understand something. This wasn't the kind of thing Millie would do. Katie's mama wasn't that kind of woman, but your papa touched her heart. He felt alone during that time, like he wasn't enough of a man. You understand that?"

Fighting emotion, Ford managed a shrug.

"And when she got pregnant, Millie was going to tell your papa. They were good friends, and what happened between them, while it was wrong, was also out of compassion. Millie was never sorry for it. She had a great gift for sharing with other people. She could feel their suffering as if it was her own."

"Katie, too," Ford said.

Carefully assessing Ford, Jack finally seemed to see

something in his new son-in-law he liked. "You love her, don't you? Katie, I mean."

Ford thought so. What he didn't know was if he loved her enough, or in the right way. "I married her."

Jack offered a slight nod, then returned to the conversation. "Before Millie could tell your papa about the baby, she found out your mama had conceived. It was gossip around the hospital, you know, since your mama had come in for a pregnancy test. So, when Millie found out they'd finally been blessed with a child of their own…" Jack's eyes settled on him. "Well, me and Millie tied the knot, and I've been a papa to Katie. All the way, she's my baby girl. But, like I said, with y'all married, it seems right that you know the truth."

It would take a lifetime, Ford figured, for the shock to wear off. "I guess so."

"Gotta say it," Jack agreed. "It's an amazing way to meet a son-in-law, but then God has some mighty mysterious ideas."

Before Jack began sermonizing as Katie said he often did, Ford added, "So, my father never knew?"

Jack shook his head. "Katie, neither. Me and Millie kept it a secret."

Their eyes met and held, and Ford felt a rush of respect. Jack was strong—physically, mentally, morally. Katie had a hell of a family.

Jack frowned. "I can't let my girl's husband know something she don't know about her own self. You understand that?"

Ford considered. The revenge he'd sought was in his power. Blood tests would reveal that Katie was

David's biological daughter, which meant Ford and Katie's baby was a blood Carrington. Legally, they were entitled to the trust, the withdrawal of which would break the foundation and bring about Ford's father's humiliation.

Ford had the trump card. But revenge suddenly didn't seem so sweet. All he wanted was Katie—and Katie's happiness. When he finally spoke, his words were deliberate, measured. "I'd like to ask a favor."

"What?"

"Can we wait to tell her?"

Jack's eyebrows rose and deep lines furrowed across his forehead. "Why?"

"It's a long story." To explain the difficulties, Ford would have to tell Jack about the baby, something better left to Katie. "Let's just say I'd like some time to settle into our lives before upsetting things."

"ARE YOU SURE my son headed toward the nursery?" David Carrington pointed down a hallway, then nervously straightened the lapels of a gray suit jacket. "Where else might I look?"

"Try his wife's office."

"Of course." As the duty nurse rattled off directions, David glanced around, then headed in the direction she indicated, but it was hard to maneuver. Maitland Maternity was in a state of pandemonium, the halls crowded with employees, their voices lowered in hushed whispers. Every time he turned a corner, David caught another snippet of gossip. The Maitland family was in trouble again.

"And I thought we Carringtons had it bad," David muttered under his breath, bracing himself to see his new daughter-in-law, Katie. He felt badly for not having congratulated her on the marriage. But how could he?

Yvonne was far too accepting. For all they knew, Katie Topper was a gold digger, or had loose morals or a checkered past that might come back to haunt them. Why couldn't Ford understand the implications of the woman's iron-clad prenuptial agreement? David winced. If Ford discovered he'd hired a private investigator to check into Katie's background, he'd be furious. Not that it mattered, since Ford was so hell-bent on taking his family to court and destroying the foundation. Besides, the initial report had contained only Katie's vital statistics.

Suddenly, a beefy, liver-spotted hand clamped on David's arm, and David smiled when he saw the burly, white-haired man attached. "Afternoon. If it isn't Cecil Nelson."

"Why, son of a gun." The elongated vowels of Cecil Nelson's speech brought back the good old days at Texas General. "If it ain't the richest doctor this side of the Mason-Dixon line." Cecil looked him over from head to foot, then ran a finger along the collar of his lab coat. "Let me tell you," he drawled, "when I retire next year, the first thing I want is a suit like yours." Before David could respond, he added, "Did you hear the news?"

David nodded, feeling a strange mixture of fear and worry. He hated to hear bad news about anyone, and this was even worse, since he knew so many of the Maitlands. "I heard some gossip as I came in the hospital, but the facts were unclear. I was looking for my son, and I thought I'd find out more from him."

"What I heard—" Cecil narrowed his eyes, so his bushy white eyebrows met above his nose "—was that Beth Maitland's ex-fiancé, a man named Dumont, married somebody else, and now the woman's been found strangled. I'm not sure, but I think her name was Brianne."

David thrust a hand anxiously through his hair, lifting and displacing gray strands. "Strangled," he repeated, racking his mind. The names sounded vaguely familiar. "After all these years in medicine, you'd think I'd feel immune to death, wouldn't you, Cecil?" Even worse, this was murder.

"Maybe more so than a civilian. Besides, we're older, David, so we're much closer to the beast."

He *was* aging. Suddenly, there seemed to be so little time. David's footsteps sped up, as did Cecil's, as if the two elderly men had jointly decided that life was short and they'd better hurry. David shook his head, suddenly wondering if he'd die without really knowing Ford. The failure of that relationship was the great failure of his life. Forcing his mind to the present, he said, "What a horrible thing to have happen. Did they arrest the man?"

Cecil shrugged. "It might not be a man. Haven't you noticed? It's equal rights these days. The body was found in Beth Maitland's office, right here in the day care."

David nodded. "In the hospital? Did they arrest anyone? Who's in charge of the case?"

"Ty Redstone." Cecil lowered his voice. "And no arrests have been made yet. They're saying Beth's a prime suspect, though." Before Cecil said goodbye and veered into a patient's room, he added, "Redstone's calling it a crime of passion."

*Passion.* Within moments David's mind shifted to his troubles. Whenever there was tension between him and Yvonne, he realized, it called up the past and the memory of his one infidelity. Yvonne had come to terms with the affair shortly after he'd told her, but she always used it as an example of how he ran from emotion in his family when he was confused. She was right, of course. Why was it so difficult to give some small sign that he cared for Ford? Why were he and his son marked with such pride?

Ford wasn't in Katie's office. Neither was Katie. Maybe it was just as well. David didn't have the slightest idea where things in their lives had gone wrong, or what to say. All the emotion in his life had come from Yvonne.

And Millie.

He smiled sadly for the woman he'd turned to so long ago, then his gaze landed on a medical thriller of the sort Ford read. Maybe his son had been in Katie's office. If she returned, what should David say?

For a moment, he stared through the window, his mind filling with words he'd never speak. *Ford, you're my boy. My first son. But I didn't know what to do, how to play with you. I still don't. By the time you came along, your grandfather, my father, had given up his medical practice, and he'd play tag with you, chasing you through the gardens. From the window, I'd watch you run through the trees, quick as summer, fast as the breeze, the wind flowing through your dark hair that's so unlike mine or your mother's.*

*But I felt like an old man already, worried about business, just like my father. And his father before him. All of us, old clocks winding down, son. All of us so worried about the Carrington name, about our own slice of immortality. Now I imagine my dying day, how the last glimmer of light will shine through the windows of Lincoln's Landing and how I'll join him. I wonder if you'll be there on that day, Ford, standing beside my bed.*

Shaking off the disjointed thoughts, David glanced around Katie's office, noticing how neatly she kept it. In one corner of her desk was a grouping of photos—pictures of a farm and three rugged-looking men, most likely her father and brothers.

*And Millie?*

Everything inside David Carrington stilled.

An eight-by-ten black-and-white photograph of Millie was prominently displayed and signed, as if she were a movie star, *For Katie to remember me by always, love, Mama.*

Mama? Was his new daughter-in-law really Millie McDean's grown child? He couldn't believe it, nor that he was seeing Millie's face again. He'd spotted her only twice since their affair. Once, pulling out of a grocery store parking lot, smiling as she talked to the children in the back seat, then years later, across a crowded movie theater. It was Yvonne who'd brought him the obituary when she died during a flu epidemic. She'd had more freckles than any man could ever count, a fiery disposition he could see in her girl, Katie, and a smile that had always aroused tenderness. He'd never love a woman as he did Yvonne, but he'd always have feelings for Millie.

"Katie's mother, though?" he whispered. The strangeness of it was still washing over him when he gasped. Katie's birth date had been among the vital statistics the investigator had given him, and as it registered, David's knees weakened. He lowered himself into Katie's desk chair.

"No…" It couldn't be true. He thought back to that time, to the treatments he'd been undergoing to help Yvonne conceive. It had also been the time when he had turned to Millie for comfort, when the beautiful young nurse had bolstered his wounded male pride. The dates were engraved in his mind…and the implications were staggering.

Katie was his daughter. His and Millie's.

Was Katie's father aware? Obviously, Ford and Katie didn't know the truth. Otherwise, Johnny Newman wouldn't be preparing to go to court. David turned, staring through the window where sunlight glanced off cars in the parking lot. No, if Ford knew the truth, he'd know the baby's trust fund was already legally theirs. He would have taken it.

Anger rushed through David. "Because he wants to destroy me."

But David held a key that could alter the future for all of them. If Ford found out the truth, the foundation and everything David had worked for over the years would be ruined. He'd lose everything.

Or gain a son.

What should he do?

## CHAPTER TEN

"THANK YOU for giving me a moment of your time."

Why had he been asked here? Ford wondered, bracing himself for whatever was to come. His eyes scanned his father's study, searching for clues. Casually dressed in slacks and a burgundy V-neck sweater, David was seated at his desk; Yvonne was standing behind him, her expression unreadable, a tight French twist and banker-gray jumper making her look severe. *Not a good sign.* Leaning back on the red-velvet-upholstered love seat he and Katie had shared a few short weeks ago, Ford relaxed a hand on the knee of his hospital pants.

Over his father's shoulders, through the tall windows, he could see trees on the front lawn, and he remembered how his grandfather used to chase him around them. Sometimes Ford would think his father was watching from the study windows, then he'd decide it was wishful thinking, nothing more than dark, fleeting shadows of sunlight glancing off glass. This morning, there was no sun. Storm clouds raced across a gray sky in fanciful shapes.

"Whatever it is must not be that important," Ford began, "seeing as Gil's not here."

David surveyed him a long moment. "Gil?"

"Your watchdog," he reminded dryly. "Blane's

father. The man you think's going to step in and save the foundation. Wasn't that why you and Mother were so approving of Blane?''

David's eyes narrowed, and Ford could see his mother's hand tighten on his shoulder. Like Gil, she was always protecting him. Before he'd talked to Jack, Ford had seen her and Gil as pawns, moved by his father at will, but now he realized they were shields, making sure no one got too close. Glancing away, Ford frowned, watching tree branches sway, brushing the windows as the first raindrops splattered across the panes. Over the years, he'd thought of his father as many things, but never weak. The revelation hurt somehow. In reality, his father was an old man. Deep grooves bracketed his mouth, wrinkles crowded his eyes, and the blue irises had faded. His father's hair, as far back as Ford could remember, had been silver.

''No,'' David finally said with a nod, ''Gil's not here.'' The wood of his desk was so polished that when he lifted a file, Ford saw the reflection. ''Johnny Newman says you're going to take me to court,'' his father began. ''That you're going to contest my father's will in an effort to secure the trust fund for your and Katie's baby.''

Ford's frown deepened at the unexpected gentling of his father's voice when he said Katie's name. He met his father's gaze. ''Do you blame me?''

David swallowed hard. ''No. I...haven't been the father I wanted to be, but just hear me out.''

''I'm listening.'' Despite the line about David's parenting abilities, Ford knew it would be a mistake to show vulnerability. If his father truly cared for him, he would have offered some gesture of reconciliation before now. He'd been given an opportunity at the party. The truth was, Ford had no family, only the one he wanted to start with Katie. He had to let go and get on with his life, but his need to feel loved by these people kept him coming back. People, as it turned out, who weren't even blood relations. How would Katie take it, he wondered, when she learned the news that she was a Carrington?

His father was weighing the folder in his hand.

"You haven't recognized my wife or my coming child," Ford found himself saying, though he'd already decided to drop the case. "So, you do understand why I'd take you to court?"

"Yes." His father's face was a stoical mask. "I don't blame you, Ford. That's why I'm telling you that you don't have to."

Patting the hand Yvonne had rested on his shoulder, David rose, looking oddly formal as he squared his shoulders and circled the desk. He handed the file folder to Ford, then crossed to the other side of the room and stood next to the window, staring at the rain.

Slowly, Ford turned the cover, wondering what new horror his father was about to unleash. Looking down for a long moment, he decided this had to be some trick. What angle was he missing? He kept his voice level. "What's this?"

"Some new information came to light."

There was nothing in the folder Ford didn't already know. In addition to an investigator's report, there was a document signed by David, saying Katie was his daughter. "I see," Ford said noncommittally.

David stared at him. "You're not surprised?"

*Maybe. But I'm not about to let it show.* "I was raised in a family where we didn't show much emotion."

Sighing, David glanced at Yvonne. "Years ago, I had an affair," he said, lowering his voice as if the words still pained him. "Your mother's known for a long time. It never happened again. I'm not a philanderer. Katie, your wife, was the result of that affair. I didn't know it until yesterday, but she's my daughter...my biological daughter." He paused, allowing Ford to glance over the written statements.

When Ford looked up, his father had turned once more toward the window, and Ford took it as a dismissal. Whatever his father's motivations, the conversation was over, and Ford felt oddly bereft. While he hated the competitiveness that characterized this relationship, it seemed that, by offering this information, his father was laying down the gauntlet. That could mean only one thing: he wanted no relationship at all. He'd handed his precious foundation over to Ford by giving Ford the legal wherewithal to bankrupt it. Maybe that's how much he wanted Ford out of his life.

Just as he turned to go, Ford softly said, "I already knew."

His father turned toward his mother, and even though both were masters at controlling their emotions, they looked surprised. His father murmured, "Knew? When?"

"A few days ago." Before anyone could respond, he added, "I don't know why you called me here, not

Katie. After all, she's your daughter, but I appreciate your letting me tell her.''

With that, he turned, and he was already gone when his father whispered, "He knew, Yvonne. He knew all along. That means he wasn't really taking us to court. Legally, he knew the money belonged to the baby already. Maybe he doesn't want to destroy me.''

Yvonne gently brushed the gray hair from his temples. "Ford never wanted to destroy the foundation, David. He just wants your attention. And now, given what you did, it's only a matter of time until he realizes how much you love him…that you were willing to give up the foundation for him."

"I hope so, Yvonne. I really hope so."

THE RAIN was coming in torrents, and as a loud crack of thunder sounded, Katie flung the lawyer's letter onto the bed, feeling furious. She'd been packing to move into Ford's bedroom when she'd found it, and she gasped, pressing a hand to her heart. "Ford," she said, finding herself face-to-face with him. "You scared me.''

"A letter came from Johnny Newman?''

"What do you think? It's right there on the bed." She shoved a hand into the back pocket of her jeans, then changed her mind and withdrew it. "If you expect me to apologize for opening your mail, don't hold your breath. I already knew what it was. I just had to see it with my own eyes."

He looked stunned. "And now you're leaving me?''

"Maybe I should.''

"You said you would if I took this to court, but I

didn't believe you.'' Ford eyed the packed Samsonite, which she'd already put by the door, and she felt her heart skip a beat. No man should look so good in baggy hospital greens, she decided, temper mixing with pure temptation. All her muscles tensed for flight. She figured his did, too. Long and hard, his leg muscles were plainly visible through cloth; chest hair that felt like velvet poured from the V-neck shirt. *Ford Freeland Carrington,* she thought. As far as she was concerned, he had no right to tempt a woman at a time like this, something that raised her temper another notch. Last night, she'd known he could be everything she wanted, but he could obviously also be vindictive.

He looked as if he meant to come across the room.

Swiftly, she raised a hand, holding it out, palm up. ''Stay there for the moment, okay?''

''Why?''

''Because if you come over here, we might wind up in this bed, just like last night.''

''Something wrong with that, Katie?''

''Right now, I might regret it. You said you'd let this court case go, try to make up with your family. You promised.''

''After last night—'' He blew out a sigh. ''I can't believe you were leaving.''

''I wasn't leaving,'' she admitted. ''I was moving to your room.''

Taking a deep breath, he leaned too casually in the door frame, his eyes watchful and sober, the grim set of his mouth a thousand times sexier than she wanted to notice. He had a file folder in his hand—from work, she imagined—and he glanced at the legal papers on the bed again. "I wasn't going through with it, Katie. I've called Johnny to tell him we're not going to court. You're right, even if we've become estranged, they're still my family. Besides, we've got plenty for the baby. Between my salary and investments, we're more than fine."

"You decided not to take your parents to court just because of me?"

"I want to do what makes you happy."

Anger heightened her color, and she felt it coursing through her, warming her body. "I don't want you to act like a good person to please me. Don't you have any compassion for your father? What about all the good work done by the foundation? Don't you get it? Your family keeps making overtures, and you choose to take every one of them the wrong way."

"Maybe you're right—" He looked distracted. "Anyway, you're my family now, Katie."

The words made her heart soar, but not enough to quell her discomfort. Maybe it was nerves. After all, once she moved down the hallway, she was committing to make this marriage last. She loved Ford, she had for years, but she was scared.

He was staring at her, those challenging dark eyes thoughtful. Weighing the folder in his hand, he started toward her. "Katie," he said, his voice lowering huskily as he neared. "I've got something to show you. It's…" His voice trailed off.

The next moments were a blur. Later, when she was far away, wet and shivering from the rain, she'd remember how he had pulled her down next to him on the bed and showed her the contents of the folder. Later, after she was wrapped in her papa's embrace telling herself she was glad Ford was out of her life, she'd contemplate his selfishness in telling her.

"My father?" she'd whispered when Ford was finished talking, her voice strangled and her heart filling with a strange mixture of terror and heartbreak. *Does Jack know? This'll kill my papa. Ford, how could you say this?* "David Carrington had an affair with my mother?" she mumbled, barely able to register the crazy words. "David Carrington? The man who raised you? He's…"

"He's your father, Katie. The trust fund's legally ours."

"Legally ours?" She gasped.

"But we're not taking it, okay? We're not going to hurt him or the foundation. I've known we could take it without contesting my grandfather's will. I'm not saying this to please you. I'd already decided not to go to court." He glanced away, toward where a sudden streak of lightning flashed on rain running down the window in rivulets. "I don't know if I'll ever have a relationship with him, Katie. But I won't hurt him or my mother." His eyes met hers again. "It's a lot to process, but your papa wants you to know the truth now."

Through tears, she saw the dark fierceness that had claimed his gaze and how his hard, strong jaw had set with determination. Under other circumstances, she might have been touched, but she felt another sting of fury at his pride. "You're more a true Carrington than you'll ever know," she accused.

He looked taken aback. "What?"

She gaped at him. "Who do you think you are?"

"Your husband, Katie."

"You're just like your parents!" she exclaimed, clamping her teeth together so he wouldn't see her chin quiver and feeling as if her whole world was coming apart. "Right now, you're doing to me exactly what your parents did to you, Ford! Without warning or preparation, you just drop a bombshell like this. You're telling me this to prove your point, with no regard for how the information will affect me."

"Oh, Katie, I'm sorry."

"Except this time," she rushed on, "it's not your father saving his precious foundation. No, this time, it's to prove your love. Damn it, Ford, love's about the *other person,* not yourself! Can't you remember how you felt the day when your folks told you that you were adopted?"

"Lousy," he admitted.

"You were a wreck!" And now she was, her whole world shifting on its axis. The man who'd loved her, held her, wiped her tears...he wasn't really her papa? She tried to ignore how Ford's damnable male heat called to her, whispering beside her in a soft rustle. "And what about my papa?" she said in a strangled voice. "What about Jack?" She could die from the pain slicing through her.

"He knows, Katie," Ford said. "He told me. My mother knows about the affair, too. I went out to see your brothers, and your father was there. The boys had told him we were married, and when he found out who I was, he..." A soft curse punctuated his speech as if Ford had just realized his best laid plans had run afoul. "Katie, I wasn't looking to hurt you. I wasn't looking to drop a bombshell—"

"No, you were just shaking up my world to prove your point."

"Katie—"

"You said you loved me last night. But you didn't even think about me just now. And my papa," she whispered. "We should have been together when I found out."

"Damn it, Katie, I didn't—"

But she was gone. She bolted, grabbing the folder, then her suitcase on the fly. A strangled sob sounded as she fled downstairs, then the hard angry slam of the door.

STARING FROM A WINDOW on the upstairs landing, Ford watched her heave the suitcase into the trunk of her car. He could barely see her through the rain, just her drenched hair, which was plastered to her head. "Oh, Katie," he whispered, feeling a rush of self-loathing. What he'd done was unthinkable; she was right. Even though he'd been crushed by the same kind of information, he hadn't put himself in her shoes. But it was too late. He watched her hop into the car and race down the driveway.

*Come back, Katie.*

Didn't she know she'd breathed new life into Lincoln's Landing the night she'd announced their marriage? That everything she touched, just like their coming child, was infused with her spirit? That she'd shaken his world? Truth was, he'd never even deserved her. He'd only shared this much of her life because their spark of passion led to a pregnancy. Thinking of the baby, Ford uttered a string of expletives, then considered his next move. No way in hell was Katie Carrington walking out of his life. Maybe he didn't deserve her. But he loved her.

"Oh, God," he whispered. "I do. I love her." But his very selfish attempt to set things right had backfired. Surely, she'd give him another chance.

*The way you gave your father another chance today?*

She was gone, but he heard her voice in the silence of the stair landing. And the voice was right. Today, had Ford only chosen to hear, it was clear his father had offered the gift of his love. He hadn't known Ford had learned of Katie's true parentage; he'd placed the means in Ford's hands to destroy the foundation he loved.

Now with Katie, Ford had meant to prove his love, but he'd been unfeeling. *You're more like your father than you'll ever admit.* Once more, it was Katie's voice.

It pained him to admit it, but it was true. Staring at the slashing rain, Ford considered calling Jack to tell him Katie was on her way. She'd go there, not to the apartment. Instead, Ford watched the dark, angry clouds racing like thieves across the sky as if they'd stolen something precious. Suddenly, the sky turned black, thrusting the landing into darkness. Reaching down, Ford pulled the bubble chain of a lamp.

As the light snapped on, he thought of his father's need, all these years, to keep a light on in Lincoln's old room. Twenty-six years was a long time to keep on a light. What loss he must have felt. How amazing that he'd managed to hide so many emotions. His hand still on the chain, Ford thought, *There, just in case.* The light was on, should Katie come home.

Something registered in Ford's mind then. Earlier, when he'd parked behind his parents' house, he'd glanced at his old bedroom. He hadn't acknowledged it at the time, but even then, he'd realized another light was burning at Lincoln's Landing now: his own.

Yeah, his father loved him, and maybe now, his father could help Ford get Katie back.

HALFWAY TO THE FARM, she realized that's where she was heading, not to her apartment. She also realized tears weren't blurring her vision so much as the fact that she wasn't using wipers, and she flicked them on. As they swiped away rain and wet leaves, it was as if a curtain was being drawn back on a vision of dark pestilence. Dangerously swaying trees blew wildly, their trunks bending, the sound buffeting the car while gutters flooded, clogging with debris. Listening to water gush under the tires, she suddenly understood she was drenched and shivering. She was still clutching the folder in her hand when she braked in front of the farmhouse and ran inside, forgetting to shut the car door because she was so anxious to reach her papa. By the time he was hugging her, she didn't even know why she was crying—because of what she'd heard or the fact that Ford had told her for his own reasons.

"There now, baby," Jack soothed, letting her weep like a little girl. Unabashedly, she clung to his waist, rubbing her cheek against his warm, soft flannel shirt, desperately needing the protective strength of the big burly arms that squeezed her tight. "I should have told you, Katie," he whispered. "But with your mama gone, I figured it was best left alone. I thought

it could have hurt the man's family, since he didn't
know about you then. And from the beginning, especially with me and your mama so in love and waiting for you, planning for you to come, it never
seemed like you could belong to any man but me."

She calmed as her papa told his side of the story,
and she swallowed around the aching knot lodged in
her throat as his huge, pawlike hand slowly rubbed
her back, just the way it had when she was a little
girl awakened by bad dreams or illness. "You're my
baby girl, Katie. You've always been, always will be.
Don't you ever forget it."

She nodded solemnly, relief flooding her. She'd
known her papa would say exactly the right thing, he
always did, and even though she was a grown woman,
she whispered in a strained voice, "Promise? You're
my papa?"

"I sure am, Katie," he whispered, splaying his fingers so wide that they seemed to cover her whole
back. "Just like Jem and Gary are always gonna be
your little brothers. Remember how you used to take
care of them after your mama died, saying you intended to be the best big sister in the whole world?
Almost like a mama? Remember how that was your
first big ambition in life?"

She nodded, rubbing her damp forehead against his
chest, relaxing in the arms that held her, her fingers
fisting at his shoulders while he told her she should
get out of her damp clothes before she caught pneu-
monia. She didn't move, though, only clung until anger claimed her again. Leaning back, she stared, the
hard, furious blinking of her eyes making tears splash

down her cheeks, mixing with the rain still falling from her hair.

"And this thing with...with his father..." Her voice trailed off, her heart aching with confusion. Would she be able to develop some sort of relationship with David Carrington? She couldn't imagine it. Pressing her cheek against her papa's shirt again, she'd never been more glad that he'd always belong to her. *What a blessing for him to be my father.* "He can be so cold," she whispered, thinking of Ford. "So unemotional," she added, her voice rising righteously. "You met him, Papa. You saw him. How, after all the gestures his father's made, can Ford keep being so tough on him? That's not family."

Jack pressed a kiss to the top of her head. "No, it's not family, is it, Katie?"

She shook her head, as he smoothed damp hair from her face. "I can't live like that," she announced, fresh tears in her eyes. She didn't feel as if she could live without Ford, either. "I can't start a family this way. With people not speaking to each other. With a father-in-law who's really my..." Her voice trailed off. "I just can't do this, Papa. My baby needs the kind of place you made for us here." *Warm. Loving. Totally uncomplicated. Where there's real support.*

She realized her papa's eyes had widened. "Your baby?"

She swallowed hard, and felt another rush of anger at Ford. How could he put her in the position of telling her papa this way? "I assumed he told you!"

Jack shook his head, thoughtfully chewing the inside of his cheek. "Nope, Katie, he sure didn't."

"Well, I'm pregnant. That's why we got married,

Papa. I'm going to have Ford's baby. But—'' Once more, moisture flooded her eyes, turning her father into a colorful blur. ''But maybe there's no father now.'' Lifting her chin pridefully, she expected to see compassion, but her papa had gotten that stern look of his, the kind he got when they were late for Sunday service.

''Lord in heaven, Katie,'' he said, ''this changes everything. Besides, you're completely overreacting.''

Licking her lips nervously, she was faintly aware they tasted salty from tears. Fighting a shiver, she wondered what her papa meant. Overreacting? She'd run here as fast as she could, knowing where she could find support. Of course, for the briefest second, she'd forgotten how religious her papa was and that her strong family values were ones he'd instilled in her personally. ''Papa?''

''Don't argue with me, Katie.'' He shook his head. ''No girl of mine will leave the father of her baby.''

# CHAPTER ELEVEN

TWO HOURS LATER the rain was still coming down in torrents. Swinging open the front door, Jem resituated a grocery bag on his hip and strode into the living room, smiling encouragement at Katie, who was curled on the couch. A quilt, which she was sharing with myriad dogs and cats, was cuddled around her shoulders, and she was wearing one of Jem's red union suits and a pair of her papa's thermal socks.

"Katie?" Jem peered as he passed to get a better look at her. "We're back. Are you still okay?"

"I'm not on suicide watch. Remember, I'm a nurse," she added, mustering a smile as she blinked eyes that were red-rimmed. "I should know."

Looking unconvinced, Jem hovered a moment longer as if he wasn't sure he should leave her side long enough to put away the groceries. "Gary's right behind me. He's shaking out the umbrellas."

"Not anymore." Gary came inside and slammed the door, the tread of his cowboy boots heavy as he approached the couch, his concerned gaze drifting over granola bar wrappers and empty potato chip bags as he set down a movie from the video store. "Shouldn't you be eating something else, Katie? I mean, for the baby?"

"I'm just not in a fruit and yogurt mood, okay?"

Looking even more worried than Jem, Gary shrugged out of his jeans jacket, dug a piece of paper from the pocket of a flannel shirt and unfolded it against his chest. "They had almost everything you asked us to get."

Jem nodded, coming in and sitting on the couch next to Katie. "Except *You've Got Mail,* and *Pretty Woman.*"

That made tears spring to her eyes, and she hugged the quilt more tightly around her shoulders for comfort, then sadly petted a mutt's flank. "No *Pretty Woman*?"

Gary winced. "A customer ruined the only copy."

"They had *Romy and Michelle's High School Reunion,* though," Jem put in quickly.

Gary nodded. "And *Runaway Bride.* Can't wait to see it."

The two of them were being so sweet that her nose stung. If Steven Segal, Jean-Claude Van Damme or Bruce Willis weren't in a movie, her brothers usually wouldn't watch it. "You don't have to watch movies with me, you know," she said. "You really don't."

Gary pushed over two of the farm cats and sat next to Jem and Katie on the couch. "What are we watching now?"

"*Message in a Bottle* with Kevin Costner," Katie told him.

Gary frowned. "Doesn't the lady die in this one?"

Jem elbowed him hard. "No. They're together in spirit, Gary. So really it's a happy ending. Don't you get it?"

"Oh, yeah," Gary agreed. "Right."

When Katie glanced through the window, she could

see a glimmer of her papa's headlights approaching through the rain. While the boys were at the video store, he'd gone to pick up a pizza. "We got extra cheese, right?" she asked.

Jem nodded. "Look, Katie, why don't you call Ford?"

She swallowed around a lump in her throat. Her papa was saying she couldn't stay here, that a woman's place was with her husband; her brothers were making every effort to absorb the information that she was only a half-sister and to assure her their relationships would never change. David Carrington had called only a few moments ago, asking if they could meet whenever she was ready; she said she'd be willing but made clear she'd never take the trust for the baby. At that point, David had surprisingly done exactly what her papa had, tried to convince her to forgive Ford. Well, she thought, Ford would have to apologize first. He'd been guilty of the same thoughtlessness that he claimed characterized his family. From outside, she heard her father's car door slam, then footsteps as he splashed through puddles, running toward the house.

Just as he came in, holding out a rain-splashed pizza box and shaking water drops from his hair, the phone rang.

A moment later, Jem handed the phone to her. "It's him."

Her fingers gripped tightly around the phone receiver. "Hello?" she said as crashingly romantic music blared from the TV. "I know it's you. Jem just told me."

"I won't keep you long."

Her heart went out to him, the lack of care she professed vanishing in a blink. "Look, Ford, I'm sorry. I—"

"I've just got a small favor to ask."

"Anything." She wanted that voice to be closer, to whisper sweet nothings in her hair again, to feel its breath on her bare skin, its warmth, like sunshine, in her blood. She wanted him to deliver their baby, to be the man on the curb outside the hospital who'd help her from the wheelchair when it was time to go home.

"Can we meet at the Stone Lodge for dinner day after tomorrow?"

She'd only been to the upscale restaurant once, but recalled a rustic interior with stone walls and small cozy rooms with gas fireplaces. Glancing around the simple but comfortable living room, she wondered if Ford would ever instinctively understand what she needed. She might be a Carrington by blood, but when it came to values, she was a Topper all the way. "Sure. We should talk."

"And, Katie…"

"What?"

"Can you bring your father and brothers?"

KATIE FROWNED as she, her papa and brothers seated themselves in captain's chairs along one side of a rough-hewn, but highly polished, wide-planked oak table in a private back room of the Stone Lodge restaurant. Facing them were Gil, Blane, David and Yvonne. David had caught Katie in the hallway and initiated an awkward, painfully polite conversation that promised to turn warmer. He'd done the same

with her papa. But why was the group assembled?
Even worse, the others didn't seem confused at being
summoned; it was as if they knew what was going
on.

She shifted nervously in her seat. She still thought
that how Ford delivered the information about David
was self-centered, but wasn't Ford trying to love her
the best way he could? Shouldn't she accept that?

Katie glanced around for clues. Barely noticeable
overhead lights were dimmed to a soft glow; candles
sparked from round glass containers, and a gas fire in
a stone fireplace released enough heat to accommo-
date the cool night.

Exhaling nervously, Katie found her manners and
managed to send Yvonne and David a weak smile.
David nodded, smiling back. Ever the social butterfly,
Blane attempted casual conversation, which fell flat
due to Katie's nervous tension.

Plastering a false smile on her face, Katie took in
the group again. Big, burly and redheaded, her papa
and brothers had come dressed in their best jeans;
they were shrugging out of work jackets, helping
themselves to rolls, which had been left in baskets.
Across the table, in dark suits and ties, Gil and David
were so motionless they could have been statues.
Long blond hair—Blane's and Yvonne's—was tightly
pulled back. The two women wore jewel-neck sweat-
ers under cardigans; Blane's was red and Yvonne's
blue.

Katie had worn the only dress she had, the sage
one in which she'd been married. Suddenly fighting
emotion, she tried not to think about the formal, burnished orange gown she'd left hanging in the closet

at Ford's. Before she could recover, she caught a glimpse of Ford in the hallway. Ignoring the hammering of her heart, she frowned when she saw the woman with him. What was Nan Rowe, the decorator, doing here? Katie recognized her from the newspaper.

Looking frazzled, Nan breezed into the room, pushing strands of windblown brown hair from her forehead. Heading toward Katie's end of the table, she dropped a portfolio to the floor, then slid into a chair next to Katie. "Katie Carrington," she gushed, finding a hand Katie wasn't even aware of offering until it was gripped with a hard squeeze. "A pleasure."

Wondering what Ford was up to, Katie said, "Likewise."

"I heard you're *the* blood Carrington!" Nan whispered, bringing a rush of Katie's temper. Where were peoples' manners? Didn't Nan understand the awkwardness of this situation? It was hardly appropriate for her to say anything, especially not with David and Yvonne sitting here. And why had Ford told Nan such sensitive information? Katie supposed it was necessary, given Nan's participation in this family gathering. She shot the Gilcrests a glance, and since they didn't seem surprised, Katie guessed David had also informed Gil. That made sense, since David's offer to deliver on the baby's trust fund affected the foundation, but *Blane* shouldn't have been told, too. Since when was Katie's life for public consumption?

A little voice answered, *Since you married Ford.*

Katie felt strangely uneasy as Ford strode into the room, carrying a stack of red-bound booklets and offering her nothing more than a quick, friendly grin. The night before last, they'd shared a bed, and he'd said he loved her. Now they could have been near strangers, still working together in the OR. When he'd called, she assumed he'd planned a private dinner. She'd been taken aback when he asked her to bring her family. But this...

Surprisingly at ease as he and his father exchanged smiles, Ford said, "Thanks for coming, everybody. I'd particularly like to thank my father. We had a long talk last night and have managed to settle some of our differences."

Katie's breath caught. What had happened between the two men? Her gaze drifted over Ford's pressed white shirt and loose-fitting tan cardigan. Lifting her gaze, she tried not to notice how light glowed in his dark hair and how shadows played on his face, accentuating deep hollows, making his features look chiseled from stone. Vaguely, she decided he was arranging various papers on the table just to torture her.

"Here," he murmured, dividing the booklets into two piles, then handing one stack to Jem and another to Gil. "Could you please pass these down? Make sure everybody gets a copy?"

Taking her booklet with far more casualness than she felt, she opened it. The first page said: Business Prospectus.

"Most of us have spoken privately, and by now, you've come to understand—" Ford paused dramatically "—that Katie and I had no choice except to marry." As he took a deep breath, Katie fought to keep from reacting. "We wanted our baby to carry on the Carrington name, and we wanted to insure, for him or her, a strong financial future...."

Feeling glad for the dark, Katie hoped no one could

see the color staining her cheeks. *There's so much more to it than that,* she wanted to cry. *We're in love, aren't we, Ford?*

Settling the red booklet on the place mat with more care than was necessary, she thrust both hands under the table, clasping them in her lap. How could he put their private business on the table? Worse, he was making it sound as if he had no feelings for her.

"The good news," he continued, "is that Katie's proven to be an asset to the Carrington Foundation. And since she's been so vocal about believing in its good works, we know she'll want to continue, though she…left me last night, and I assume she intends to maintain separate households."

Separate households! She hadn't said that!

"I've no doubt she'll agree to appear with me publicly when necessary—" Ford shot her an apologetic smile, adding, "It won't be often." To the group, he continued, "She'll act as official foundation spokesperson for us."

Aware her muscles were tightening with anger, she didn't move when he shot her another easy grin, a flash of white teeth that made her feel as if she might implode. "You did a great job promoting the Carrington Clinic, Katie," he complimented, with a wink that said this could be a fresh start for them. "You proved you could function as a Carrington."

That was rich. She was the Carrington, not him. "I *am* a Carrington."

"Yes, well…" Ford's smile broadened benevolently as he looked at Nan. "Nan, as I'm sure everybody already knows, is a well-known Austin home decorator. What you don't know about Nan is that she got her start in the art department of one of the nation's top advertising agencies, and so, because of our long association…"

While Ford went into a lengthy spiel, detailing Nan's accomplishments, Katie could barely hear for the blood rushing in her ears. By the time Ford was finished, she'd unclasped her hands and was pressing fingers to her wrist, monitoring her pulse. If it became any more rapid, she'd leave. Already, she was heading for a medical emergency.

Oblivious, Nan grinned and rose to her feet, laying drawings and sketches on the table. "Ultimately, our goal is to double the foundation's available funds. Between an ad campaign and the agreed-upon merger Ford has negotiated with the Gilcrest Endowment, we'll fund more projects, and also—" Nan shot Katie a grin "—make your baby the richest newborn in Austin."

"I'm hardly interested in the baby's trust," Katie said stiffly. "I told David that. And Ford." Wasn't anybody listening to her? And what gave Ford the right to step in and take over her life like this? Why was he making their private business public?

Smiling, Nan continued breezily. "Ford's got plenty of ideas about investing Carrington-Gilcrest capital, detailed in the prospectus in front of you." While David and Gil, who'd continued leafing through the booklets, nodded with interest, Nan said, "All those graphs and financial projections, I can't understand them myself. What I do know is advertising, and here is the logo Ford asked me to design. It'll run in print and television ads. As foundation spokesperson, Katie will be making the public appearances—''

Katie's jaw dropped. ''Public—''

''Your rallying volunteers for the Carrington Clinic got people interested,'' Nan excitedly explained. ''You'll do news interviews, local and national radio spots, ribbon cuttings, building dedications—''

''Dedications?'' Katie echoed, glaring at Ford, her voice louder than she'd intended. ''It would be nice if someone bothered to ask about my commitment!''

Everybody stared at her. Ford looked shocked. ''Do you have a problem committing yourself to a family enterprise, Katie?'' he asked.

Suddenly, she felt on the verge of tears. ''I don't even know if we're really married, Ford!''

At the outburst, the room became silent. She heard Nan put down a pencil. A water glass clinked as Jem placed it on the table. A waitress in a red-checkered shirt appeared at the door, surveyed the situation, changed her mind and left.

Ford didn't look disturbed in the least. ''You never did move into my bedroom,'' he said casually, ''if that's what you mean, Katie.''

Such deep color stained her cheeks that even the dim light wouldn't mask it. She was so mortified, she didn't dare look around the room, and yet her body was overriding her mind. It took charge, shooting her from her seat. Before she knew what was happening, she'd circled the table. She stopped in front of Ford, her voice shaking. ''We're in public, Ford!''

''True.'' A dark eyebrow rose, and he tilted his head in puzzlement. ''But it's a family business meeting, Katie. As a family, we share.''

"What are you trying to prove?"

"I thought we discussed all this."

"Oh, kiss my round Irish behind," she muttered in frustration. "And don't shoot me that innocent look," she added, taking in the boyishly parted lips she knew were so kissable, then the dark wide eyes that she'd seen smolder so often with desire. "You haven't looked so innocent since the day you were born. Now, what is it you *think* we discussed?"

"How families pull together." His expression of censure suggested she was the most self-centered person present. "This isn't just about you, Katie," Ford warned, a genuine smile tugging his lips. "My father, mother and I spent last night together, and now we're all hoping Jack can oversee construction on a new office for the foundation. Nan will decorate it. Blane and Yvonne will plan fund-raising events, while the Gilcrest endowment..."

She barely heard the rest. Somehow, his laid-back attitude was starting to hurt. "You expect me to be a *spokesperson?*" she managed to ask.

"If you don't mind."

"Mind!" she countered. "Of course I mind. I can't live like this. I can't be a spokesperson! You're saying this as if you expect me to meet you before Carrington Foundation events and enter them hanging on to your arm while smiling for the cameras! Do you really expect me to play the part of your adoring wife?"

Ford stepped nearer, and as his hands settled on her hips, she had the strangest sense he'd been goading her into this reaction all along. "No. There's another solution, Katie."

Tilting her head, she felt a rush of love such as she'd never experienced. It tunneled through her, taking her breath. He'd made up with his parents, and he'd done it for her. She was suddenly sure of it. He'd pulled this group together, swallowed his pride and given their baby all the love it deserved. "Another solution?" she managed to ask, her throat raw as the hands around her waist tightened.

"*Be* my adoring wife, Katie."

"You want me to come home tonight?"

"One night away from you was too many. I left the light on in the window for you, Carrot Top." It was a reminder that endings come too quickly, often unexpectedly, and so when the ring of love appeared, you had to grasp it.

"Be my wife, Katie," he whispered.

She lifted on her toes, curling her palms over his shoulders and seeking the firm warmth of waiting lips that would always be hers to kiss, and then she whispered the only words that were left to be said. "I'm already your wife, Ford Carrington."

THAT SPRING, while the Topper men worriedly paced the halls of Maitland Maternity and Yvonne and David anxiously sipped coffee in the hospital cafeteria, Katie gave birth to a daughter. Delivered by her own papa, Mildred Yvonne Carrington was two weeks early. She was born with a square Carrington jaw, a tuft of bright red Topper hair and a generous, toothless grin that announced she was, from her very first breath, the healthiest, happiest, richest little baby girl in Texas.

*MAITLAND MATERNITY*
continues with
*THE DETECTIVE'S DILEMMA*
*by Arlene James*

*Beth Maitland might be a little more conventional
than the rest of the Maitland clan, but she never
dreamed she'd find herself framed for a murder she
didn't commit. Then she discovered that the detective
working on her case was sexy-as-sin Ty Redstone.
And suddenly, Beth couldn't help wishing she'd taken
up a life of crime earlier....*

*Available in February
Here's a preview!*

# CHAPTER ONE

*"YOU BELIEVE ME?" Beth asked incredulously.*

Ty smiled self-deprecatingly. "Let's just say I have a nose for a frame-up and a very open mind."

Relief percolated inside her, making her feel suddenly giddy. "So you think Brandon's framing me?"

Ty bowed his head. "Problem is, I can't prove it," he said matter-of-factly, stepping up to the end of the table. "Yet."

Suddenly, Beth's arms were around his neck. "Thank you! Oh, thank you! You don't know what a relief it is to—" She realized abruptly that she'd wrapped herself around him. She noticed, too, that his heart was beating every bit as rapidly as her own. He was trying to keep his distance—and not completely succeeding.

Ty cleared his throat and gingerly brought his hands to hers, gently disengaging her arms as he pushed her away.

"Sorry," she mumbled, very aware that he wasn't looking at her. Instead, he was focusing on the folder that he had left on the table. "I suppose that sort of thing happens all the time," she said, hearing the husky tenor in her own voice.

"Uh, no, actually. That's, uh, that's a first."

Beth was oddly pleased. "Really."

He nodded and flipped open the folder. One hand drifted up to rub at the corner of his eye. "I'm usually considered kind of, oh, unapproachable."

"Unapproachable?" she echoed disbelievingly. "You?" He shot her a warning look, and she sensed a challenge. She shook her head. "Uh-uh. No, that's not how I'd describe you at all."

"No? And how would you describe me, then?"

Beth knew she was being audacious, but she didn't care. "Personable. Sexy. Drop-dead gorgeous."

His mouth dropped open. Then he coolly folded his arms and tried to change the subject. He cleared his throat. "Listen, in regard to the case, Ms. Maitland, I don't want you to worry. We'll get to the truth."

"Beth," she corrected.

"What?"

"Call me Beth. There are a number of Ms. Maitlands. I'm Beth."

He shook his head. "Okay, I don't want you to worry, Beth."

Pleased, she responded primly. "I'll try not to, Ty." She leaned forward slightly. "I may call you Ty, may I not?"

His lips twitched with what could have been a smile. "I suppose so."

The light of interest fairly smoldered in his eyes, but he was working hard to suppress it. Only she didn't want him to suppress it. Placing both hands on the tabletop, she leaned closer to him. "Now who's unapproachable?" she teased huskily. "I don't think you're unapproachable. I think you're more of a magnet."

A slow grin spread across his face, and he leaned down, bringing his nose close to hers. "And I suppose there's iron beneath that sweet, feminine exterior of yours."

"Must be," she murmured, as their lips met.

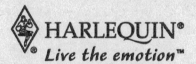

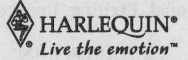

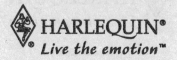

 **Harlequin Historicals®**
Historical Romantic Adventure!

*From rugged lawmen and valiant knights to defiant heiresses and spirited frontierswomen, Harlequin Historicals will capture your imagination with their dramatic scope, passion and adventure.*

*Harlequin Historicals . . . they're too good to miss!*

# HARLEQUIN®
## *Presents*

**The world's bestselling romance series...
The series that brings you your favorite authors,
month after month:**

Helen Bianchin...Emma Darcy
Lynne Graham...Penny Jordan
Miranda Lee...Sandra Marton
Anne Mather...Carole Mortimer
Susan Napier...Michelle Reid

## and many more uniquely talented authors!

Wealthy, powerful, gorgeous men...
Women who have feelings just like your own...
The stories you love, set in exotic, glamorous locations...

# HARLEQUIN®
## *Presents*

**Seduction and Passion Guaranteed!**

HPDIR104